Nurse Alissa vs. the Zombies VII: On the Road

Nurse Alissa vs. the Zombies VII: On the Road

Scott M. Baker

Also by Scott M. Baker

Novels
Nurse Alissa vs. the Zombies
Nurse Alissa vs. the Zombies: Escape
Nurse Alissa vs. the Zombies III: Firestorm
Nurse Alissa vs. the Zombies IV: Hunters
Nurse Alissa vs. the Zombies V: Desperate Mission
Nurse Alissa vs. the Zombies VI: Rescue
The Ghosts of Eden Hollow
Shattered World I: Paris
Shattered World II: Russia
Shattered World III: China
Shattered World IV: Japan
Shattered World V: Hell
The Vampire Hunters
Vampyrnomicon
Dominion
Rotter World
Rotter Nation
Rotter Apocalypse
Yeitso

Novellas
Nazi Ghouls From Space
Twilight of the Living Dead
This Is Why We Can't Have Nice Things During the Zombie Apocalypse

Anthologies
Cruise of the Living Dead and other Stories
Incident on Ironstone Lane and Other Horror Stories
Crossroads in the Dark V: Beyond the Borders
Rejected for Content
Roots of a Beating Heart
The Zombie Road Fan Fiction Collection

A Schattenseite Book

Nurse Alissa vs. the Zombies VII: On the Road
by Scott M. Baker.
Copyright © 2021. All Rights Reserved.
Print Edition
ISBN-13: 978-1-7351312-9-0

Cover Art © Christian Bentulan

Chapter One

MONICA SAWYER STARED intently at the computer screen sitting on top of the console, monitoring the flight of the RQ1, the reconnaissance version of the Predator UAV, as it flew fifteen feet over the train tracks. She used the joystick to keep its path steady. Fred Downes, the train's back-up engineer, stood beside Monica and studied the screen, looking for anything along or beside the tracks that might impede their progress. So far he had seen nothing. No debris. No changes to the railway switch. No hordes of deaders.

Kimberly Brown, the engineer, stood by the throttles, becoming increasingly annoyed. "How does it look?"

"So far it's clear," answered Downes. "Nothing blocking the tracks and no debris."

"What about Scavengers?"

"No signs of them either."

"Thank God."

Red Ball Three, an EMD F7 diesel engine, followed twenty miles behind the UAV but cruised at a speed of only five mile per hour, pulling along ten cars of supplies for the government installation at White Sands, including a tanker filled with distilled water. The practice had become SOP, Standard Operating Procedure, for running the supply trains between St. Louis and White Sands. The UAV would fly ahead of the train and scan for potential danger. Checkpoint Bravo was always a hot spot. Located west of Salena, Checkpoint Bravo, known before the apocalypse as Hutchinson, was a town once home to three thousand people, now three thousand deaders. It was also the point where the train would switch to a secondary rail line that bypassed the deader-infested population centers along the main lines in favor of a northern route that ran through the countryside before turning south for a run into Albuquerque. Recent reports indicated the Scavengers, an army of raiders from southern Colorado, had been spotted in the area. Checkpoint Bravo would be an ideal location for an ambush.

The UAV made its sweep of Hutchinson, passing by the train station on the left and a row of box cars seated on a siding to the right, then continued to the junction. Downes leaned forward and studied the monitor. The railway switch indicated the track would transfer them to the northern route.

"Perfect," he said. "We should be good to go."

"Can I fire her up?" asked Kim.

"Not yet," said Monica. "I want to do an overhead pass to make sure it's safe."

"Hurry up." Kim's tone dripped with impatience.

Monica ignored her. She maneuvered the UAV into a circle and brought it to an elevation of one thousand feet. Five minutes later, the reconnaissance drone made its second pass over Hutchinson. Neither she nor Downes spotted any deader or human activity.

"The coast is clear."

"Finally." Kim pushed forward the controller, bringing the train's speed up to thirty miles per hour. Red Ball Three made its way toward Hutchinson.

CARTER SLADE STOOD in the tower of the train station, watching the UAV pass low over the tracks. He checked his watch. Only a few minutes behind schedule. God Bless military efficiency. As it flew by, Gina Carlos turned to him.

"Should I proceed?"

Slade shook his head. "Give it a minute. If they're smart, they'll make another pass."

Five minutes later, the UAV made a second run through the area, this time at a higher altitude. He waited until it passed to the west and, once out of sight, turned to Gina.

"Give the order."

She withdrew a cellphone and dialed. A gruff voice on the other end answered, "What?"

"Go ahead."

From the station beneath them, five men led by Mauler, the former head of a local biker gang and now one of Slade's bodyguards, exited onto the tracks. Earlier that morning, they had unfastened the bolts from a section of track just beyond the station. Now they raced out and used three-foot-long crowbars to pry the rail from its mountings. It took less than five minutes for them to break it free, tip it on its side, and return to the station where they joined Slade and Gina in the tower.

Mauler spit a wad of chewing tobacco on the floor. "Done."

"Proceed with stage two," said Slade.

Gina dialed a second number. A female voice answered. "My turn?"

"Yes."

Yvette Tyler emerged from under one of the box cars sitting on the siding and climbed to the top. She ran down to a chain latched to the roof, unwound the end from its mooring, and pulled it toward the rear of the car, opening the side door. Fifty deaders tumbled out, climbing to their feet and spreading out across the tracks. Each had a collar made of primer chord wrapped around its neck and held together by a detonator control box. Two lights were attached to the latter, one green and one red. The red light glowed.

Once the deaders had sauntered across the track, Gina dialed a third number.

"Yes?" asked Toni Candolini, the head of the assault team.

"Everything's set. Be ready to move."

"Roger that," replied Tony.

Gina closed the phone and slid it back in her pocket. "Everything is in place."

Slade smiled. "Now we wait."

MONICA AND DOWNES kept their attention focused on the screen as the UAV flew over the tracks along the northern route the train would soon be taking. They were only distracted when Kim yelled, "Fuck!"

"What's wrong?" asked Downes.

"There's a pack of deaders on the track."

Monica peered out the front window. "Impossible. They weren't there a few minutes ago."

"They are now." Kim pushed the controller forward. The train picked up speed.

Downes joined her. "What are you doing?"

"There's not that many. I'm going to push my way through them."

Before Downes could protest, the engine slammed into those deaders on the track, numbering close to twenty. Their bodies shattered on impact with one hundred and twenty-five tons of steel, splattering the windows and front end in congealed blood and body parts.

"Serves those motherfuckers—"

Red Ball Three reached the section of track that had been sabotaged. The engine swung left onto solid ground, lost control, and tumbled onto its left side. Monica and Downes were thrown against the left slide of the cab. Kim flew out of the engineer's seat, slamming her head on the console and being thrown against the rear of the cab. The screeching of metal against dirt and rails drowned the panicked screams of those inside the cab. The engine slid across the ground until it collided with another diesel engine abandoned on a siding.

Each of the box cars lost control. The first three went off the track and landed at different angles. One burst open, sending packages of MREs across the dirt. The last seven overturned, falling sideways onto the station platform. The ten-man private security detail in the caboose were not prepared, being tossed around. Those not wounded or knocked unconscious, seven in total, climbed out of the wreckage to see what happened.

They were immediately set upon by the remaining deaders. Gunfire erupted around the derailed train as the security team battled the living dead. Normally the highly trained team would have no problem taking down this number of deaders but, being disoriented and dazed by the derailment, they were not on their game. Twelve deaders went down before rest of the pack descended on the survivors. Three of them took down the closest member of the team, tearing him apart in their frenzy for food. Four more dropped to their knees to feed. The rest descended onto the remaining members of the team.

During the melee, no one noticed that twenty-five Scavengers jump out of the right side of one of the boxcars on the siding and climb onto the roof. Once they were in place, Tony called Gina.

"We're in position."

IN THE CONTROL tower, Gina answered the call. She turned to Slade.

"They're all set."

Slade withdrew a detonator from his pocket and flipped the switch.

THE RED LIGHT on each of the deaders' collars switched to green and the rolls of primer chord around their necks detonated. The largest explosion occurred around the security member being devoured, the combined explosives ripping apart the seven deaders and their victim, scattering body chunks and gore across the area, some splashing on the Scavengers standing on top of the sidelined boxcar. One young woman pinned by a deader against an overturned box car died in the blast, the front of her face and chest being torn off. Two other security personnel near the pack suffered severe injuries, one blinded by shrapnel and the other receiving multiple wounds to his face and neck.

As suddenly as the carnage had started it ended. An unsettling calm settled over the area, disturbed by the sound of automatic weapons being cocked. The security detail looked up at the box car, realizing they had lost the advantage. One member raised his weapon to fire and was cut down by three of the Scavengers, their bullets turning his upper body into pulp. The others froze in terror as the shredded corpse dropped onto the track.

"Anyone else want to be a fucking hero?" asked Tony.

No one did.

"Smart move. Drop your weapons."

The remaining security members carefully placed their weapons on the ground.

"Now on your knees with your hands behind your head."

They obeyed.

As five of the Scavengers kept their weapons trained on the prisoners, the rest climbed down, some checking on the rest of the security team in the caboose, the others climbing onto the derailed box cars and checking the contents.

Tony called Gina.

"The area is secure."

ON GETTING THE go ahead, Slade exited the tower, Gina and the others joining him. Once in the train station, he exited onto the platform and made his way through the derailment to the other side. Upon seeing the boss, Tony raced over to greet him.

"What's the take?" Slade asked.

"My people are still checking, but so far we have a box car of MREs, one with clothes, and three with equipment of some type, probably to set up agricultural and water distilling facilities at White Sands. We're checking the others now. Oh, and the tanker is filled with fresh water."

"Damn. I was hoping it would be fuel."

Tony's eyes widened. "You thought it was filled with gas and you derailed it by my men?"

Slade didn't respond, but the gaze he gave Tony clearly let the subordinate know he was out of line.

"Sorry, boss." Tony lowered his head.

"Where are the survivors?"

"We're checking the engine now. Those from the security detail are over here."

Tony led Slade and Gina to the caboose. Five men and two women knelt by the tracks. Six had their hands behind their head, the seventh raising only his left arm because the right dangled limply by his side. One was blind from shrapnel and another wounded from the detonation of the primer chords. Slade walked the line slowly, giving each of the prisoners a casual glance as he passed. He stopped in front of the last one, a young woman with auburn hair terrified of what would happen next.

"Is this all of them?"

"Two were killed by deaders and one had his neck broken in the crash."

Slade crouched in front of the woman. She averted her gaze. Slade placed his thumb and fore finger on her chin and lifted her head until their eyes met. He smiled at her before standing.

"Call the trucks and have the men start loading them with what we need. Burn the rest. Take as much water as we can carry and drain the rest so they can't use it."

"What about the prisoners?"

Slade did not even cast them a glance. "Take the women back to camp. Shoot everyone else."

The Scavengers guarding the prisoners fired before anyone could react, each pumping five rounds into the chests of the male prisoners. As their bullet-ridden bodies collapsed, four other Scavengers moved forward and pulled the two women off their knees, herding them away. The auburn-haired woman attempted to fight back, at least until one of the guards cracked her across the face with the stock of his rifle.

Slade witnessed none of this. He had already ordered three Scavengers to follow him and headed for the front of the train. Gina ran along beside him.

"Where are we going?" she asked.

"I want to see if anyone in the engine survived."

MONICA WAITED UNTIL the engine and derailed cars had come to a stop before moving. She felt blood dripping from the back of her neck where shards of glass shattered by the impact had cut into her skin. Thankfully, her body had landed on the frame and not the window otherwise she might have been ripped apart. Kim lay a few feet from her. Monica crawled over and checked her pulse, though she didn't need to. The severe angle of Kim's neck told Monica she had broken it during the crash. Downes, who lay at the rear of the cab, groaned and rolled over, struggling to stand. He stumbled over to Monica.

"Is she...?"

"She's dead." Monica closed the woman's eye lids.

"What happened? The tracks were clear."

"Must be Scavengers. Bastards must have been waiting to ambush us. We need—" The sound of gunfire cut her off.

8

"What's that?"

"It's the security detail killing off the deaders. They can use some help. Follow me."

With Downes leading the way, the two grabbed their M4 Carbines. Detonations came from the rear of the train.

"Were we carrying explosives?"

"No," replied Downes, shaking his head. "I have no idea what that is."

The only available exit was through the engineer's door on the upturned right side of the cab. Locking his fingers together, Downes used his hands as a platform to lift Monica. She opened the door and climbed out, then leaned back in and helped Downes escape. As he pulled himself out of the cab, semi-automatic weapons fire came from the rear of the train.

"Those don't sound like our guns," said Downes.

"They're AK-47s."

The two crouched and made their way along the overturned engine, dropping down to the ground once they were free of the debris pile. Readying their weapons for combat, the two made their way toward the rear of the engine, staying close to the roof for cover. Peering around the corner, Monica motioned for Downes to proceed. He ran out, fell prone, and crawled under the coupling. Once on the other side, he waved for Monica to follow. She did. She had made it halfway under the coupling when Slade and the others came around the end of the box car. Monica was in no position to shoot, but Downes was. He aimed his M4 at Slade. The three Scavengers drew down on him.

"Enough." Slade turned to his people. "Lower your weapons."

The three Scavengers hesitated. Slade raised his hand in front of his chest and slowly lowered it. The men pointed the barrels of their AK-47s toward the ground. He shifted his gaze to Downes.

"Your turn."

"Why should I?" Downes' tone waivered.

"I have twenty-five men with me. Shoot me if you want, but then they'll gun you down, your lady friend, and the rest of the prisoners. I'm giving you a chance to live."

He hesitated.

"Do it," said Monica. "You can't win this one."

Downes removed his finger from the trigger and left hand from the barrel. Keeping the weapon pointed above him, he laid it on the ground beside him, then carefully raised his—

Slade withdrew his Glock 23 from its holster and shot Downes in the forehead. A geyser of blood and brains erupted from the back of his skull. The body stiffened for a moment before collapsing backward.

Monica went for her M4 only to find the three Scavengers pointing their AK-47s at her.

Slade reholstered his Glock and walked away, Gina tagging along behind him.

"Take her back to camp."

One of the Scavengers stepped forward and kicked Monica in the face, knocking her unconscious.

Chapter Two

A LISSA WOKE UP slowly. She lay there, her eyes closed, as she transitioned out of sleep. After a few minutes, the constant hum and the steady, low vibrations reminded her she was aboard the Amphibious Assault Ship *U.S.S. Iwo Jima* off the coast of New England.

Alissa recalled falling asleep with a large, furry, bed-hogging bunk mate. Shithead no longer pushed her against the cold bulkhead. She reached out and felt around the mattress, but he had moved. Finally opening her eyes, she checked the floor. At some point, Shithead had abandoned her and now lay a few bunks down with Kiera, snuggling close to the teenager and snoring.

No light filtered in through the porthole, which didn't surprise her. Alissa felt like she had slept for hours. The straining in her bladder confirmed it. As she pushed aside the covers, something weighing them down caught her attention. A pair of dark blue pants and a light blue shirt sat folded on the end of the bunk along with a towel, a small bottle of shampoo, and a bar of soap, the latter two resting on top of a note. She pulled it out and read it.

Alissa,

The captain gave each of us a change of clothes. I guess we smell ripe.

Kiera

Alissa glanced down at her clothes. Ripe would be an understatement. She had become so used to be covered in deader blood she barely noticed it anymore. Her current outfit, including her boots and leather coat and pants, were soiled with the remains of the living and the living dead. Even her hands had ground in streaks of red from blood. She could use a hot shower to relax the muscles that were tight and achy from two days of combat.

Swinging her legs out of the bunk and picking up the clean clothes and toiletries, Alissa made her way to the showers. Once in the lit corridor, Alissa blinked her left eye several time. Not only had the black spot from yesterday not gone away it had grown larger, now effecting nearly twenty-five percent of her vision. She would check it out later.

Only a few people were in the showers. She stripped down and took a long, semi-warm shower. Not that it mattered. It felt good to be clean again. Judging by the amount of blood and dirt that swirled down the drain, she needed it. When finished, she slid on her old underwear and the new shirt, which fit loosely. The rest, except for the leather jacket and pants, she dumped in the trash. The jacket and pants she washed down as best she could with water from one of the sinks.

After dropping off the towel and toiletries back at her bunk, Alissa made her way to the mess hall. The breakfast line had already started to form. The aroma drifting from the kitchen made her stomach rumble. At 0500, the doors opened and the line moved forward. The cooks served scrambled eggs, bacon, and diced potatoes. She took a huge helping of each, plus an orange juice and cup of coffee. Entering the mess, she saw Patricia and Susie seated at a table, the former in dark blue pants and a light blue shirt, the latter still in what she had worn on the island. Alissa made her way over to them.

"Mind if I join you?"

Susie beamed. "Have a seat."

Alissa sat down. "How's the food?"

Susie shrugged. "It's okay, but it's not as good as IHOP."

Patricia leaned over and hugged the girl. "You must be rested."

"Why do you say that?" Alissa scooped some eggs into her mouth.

"You slept sixteen hours."

"That long?"

"You needed it."

"And you snore," added Susie.

Alissa almost spit out her eggs trying not to laugh. "Are you sure it wasn't Shithead?"

"He snores, too. But not as loud as you."

"Susie," Patricia politely chastised the girl. "You don't say things like that. It's not nice."

Susie pouted. "Sorry, Aunt Alissa."

"That's all right." Alissa leaned closer and gave Susie a conspiratorial wink. "I know it's true."

"Aunt Alissa, what's going to happen to us now?"

"I don't know."

"Kiera says you own a cabin in the woods in New Hampshire. Can we stay with you?"

With all that had gone on the past few days, she had not given much thought to what would happen after their rescue from Warren Island. She had no idea how her team would get back to North Conway.

"I think we can arrange that."

"Really?" Susie asked excitedly.

"Yes." Alissa paused. "Could you do me a favor and get me a glass of iced water?"

"Sure." Susie bolted from the table.

When she was out of earshot, Alissa leaned closer to Patricia. "I don't mind taking you both with me, but does Susie have any other family she should go to?"

Patricia shook her head. "Susie's parents had her late in life. Both sets of grandparents are dead. Her father had two brothers. One was killed in a car accident three years ago along with his entire family. The other lives in California with his family, but no one knows what happened to them since the outbreak."

"What about you?"

"My husband, Phil, died trying to save Susie's family. His parents are dead. He has a brother who lives in Arizona and a sister in Philadelphia, but we haven't heard from them. I'm an only child and my parents retired to Orlando. The chances of any of them having survived are nil. I'm all Susie has. We stick together."

"Good for you. I promise I'll take care of both of you."

"Thank you." Patricia reached out and held Alissa's hand.

Susie ran up. "I have your iced water."

"Thank you." Alissa took a long drink. The three chatted about anything they could think of except deaders. As Alissa ate, she described to Susie the cabin, Little Stevie and Connie, and Archer.

"You have a cat?"

Alissa nodded. He's a bit of an asshat, but he loves children."

"I can't wait to meet him."

"You will soon."

When the women finished breakfast, they picked up their area and placed the trays on the conveyor belt leading back into the kitchen. As they exited the mess hall, Patricia said, "Susie and I are heading back to our quarters to play with Shithead. Do you want to join us?"

"No, thanks. I need to check on Chris and Nathan."

ALISSA MADE HER way to sickbay. Stepping inside, she immediately felt at home. The medical facilities aboard the *Iwo Jima* were like those she worked with at Mass General, albeit in this case enclosed within eighteen thousand tons of steel and with much less pandemonium acquainted with a big city ER.

A corpsman sat in the waiting room in front of a computer typing away. Alissa walked over to him.

"Excuse me."

The corpsman looked up and greeted her with a smile. "How can I help you, ma'am?"

"I'm looking for my friends. They were brought in last night aboard the helicopter from Warren Island."

"You mean Patient Zero and the guy with the leg wound. They're in the recovery unit. Follow me."

The corpsman logged off, stood, and led Alissa down a corridor to a door. He paused by the opening. "They're in there, ma'am."

"Thank you."

"You're welcome. Let me know if you need anything else."

As the corpsman went back to his duties, Alissa entered.

The recovery unit consisted of twenty-three beds lined up along either side of the bulkheads. Only the two across from the door were occupied. Alissa's heart soared when she saw Nathan and Chris. They both rested with their eyes closed.

"Aren't you two a lazy pair."

Their eyes shot open. Both men grinned.

"Here I'm the one saving your miserable asses... again... and all you can do is sleep."

"Hey." Chris pointed to his wounded leg. "I was shot."

"You were hit by a ricochet. Big difference." Alissa crossed over to Chris' bed, hugged him tight, and kissed his cheek.

She stepped over to Nathan. "What's your excuse?"

"I'm special. I'm Patient Zero."

Alissa hugged Nathan and gave him a kiss.

"Where have you been all this time that you couldn't visit us earlier?" asked Chris.

Alissa felt her cheeks blush. "I was... sleeping."

"For how long?"

"Sixteen hours."

Chris glanced over at Nathan and winked. "And *we're* the lazy ones."

"It wears a girl out trying to keep the two of you alive." Alissa sat on the end of Nathan's bed. "But seriously, how are you both feeling?"

"I'm good," said Chris. "Of course, it helps they've been giving me pain killers all night."

"I've been on an IV and antibiotics since we got here." Nathan raised his right arm to show the drip needle stuck in his arm. "I feel a lot better than yesterday."

"What about Saunders?"

Chris became somber. "Between the wound and the frostbite, they had to amputate his leg. He's in ICU right now."

"Poor guy," said Alissa.

"At least he's alive," added Nathan.

Alissa pushed the thought from her mind. "So, how long are you two going to milk being sick?"

Chris placed his hands behind his head, leaned back against the pillow, and smiled. "For as long as I can."

"Which won't be long." The voice came from the doorway.

Alissa shifted on the bed to get a better view. An African-American woman centered herself in the opening. She wore a white lab coat over her khaki uniform and had her pulled back tight in a bun. Her expression was devoid of emotion.

She stepped into the room and approached Alissa. "I'm Senior Medical Officer Harris."

"I'm Alissa Madison."

"Glad to meet you. Your friend Nathan should be back to normal in a few days. He was severely dehydrated and exhausted due to the infection. I want to keep him under observation another twenty-four hours. After that, he should be fine. I'd take it easy for a while until you get your strength back."

"Good." Alissa squeezed Nathan's hand.

"If what they say about him is true, that he was infected with the deader virus and fought it off, the medical staff at White Sands will want to examine him." Harris focused her gaze on Nathan. "You could be carrying the anti-bodies to stop all this."

Nathan rolled his eyes. "Lovely."

"Wait a minute," interrupted Alissa. "I thought the blood samples we retrieved for Carrington were the source of the vaccine."

"Either one could be the miracle we're looking for." Harris reached out and patted Nathan's feet. "Thanks to you, we doubled our chances of success."

"What about me?" asked Chris.

"What about you?"

"I was shot."

Harris tilted her head to one side and frowned. "You were hit by a ricochet. I'm not putting you in for a Purple Heart."

Chris pretended to sulk.

Harris turned her attention to Alissa. "We cleaned the wound and stitched him up. He'll be fine, but it'll hurt him to walk for a week to ten days."

"Can I get some pain killers?" asked Chris.

"I'll get you some children's aspirin," the SMO responded without looking at him.

"Thank you so much for looking after them."

"That's what I'm here for, ma'am."

Alissa leaned in closer and whispered. "Do you have a place we could talk for a moment in private?"

"Follow me."

Harris led Alissa into the corridor and down to one of the examination rooms, ushering her inside. Harris closed the door.

"What can I do for you?"

"Could you check my left eye? I'm having difficulty seeing out of it."

Harris motioned for her to sit on the exam table and pulled a pen-sized flashlight from her pocket. "What's wrong with it?"

"Yesterday, a deader knocked me over and I hit my head on the gunwale of a ship." Alissa sat on the table and scooted back a few inches. "Shortly after that, a black circle began obstructing my vision."

"Lean your head back, please." When she did, Harris shown the light into Alissa's left eye. "Does the black circle float around?"

"No. It stays in the center of my vision."

"Has it changed in size?"

"It's doubled since last night."

Harris switched the light to Alissa's right eye. "Does it hurt?"

"No pain or discomfort."

Shutting off the flashlight and slipping it back into her pocket, Harris stepped back five feet. "Close your left eye and look directly at my face."

Alissa did.

Harris placed her hand in front of her face and extended her index and middle finger. "How many fingers do I have up?"

"Two."

"Switch eyes." When she did, Harris also raised her thumb. "How many fingers do I have up?"

"I can't see your face, hands, or body down to your waist."

"You can open your eyes."

"What's the diagnosis?"

Harris leaned against the bulkhead and rested her arms on her lap. "The retina has detached from the back of your left eye. The black spot is caused by visual light not reaching the sensors. The more the retina detaches, the larger the black spot will get."

"You mean it's going to get worse?"

"Within a week, you'll probably lose all vision in that eye."

Alissa tried to comprehend what the medical officer told her. It was hard enough making it through the apocalypse as is. Doing so with one eye significantly lessened her chances of survival.

"Can it be fixed?"

"It's not a major surgery. The problem is finding someone qualified to perform it and a location where it can be done."

"So, I'm going to go blind in my left eye."

Harris nodded. "I wish I could do something to help. The only saving grace is that the effects will be isolated to your left eye. It's not an infection or a tumor that could spread. But I know that's not much comfort."

"I appreciate you taking a look at it."

"My pleasure." Harris searched through the various cabinets on the wall before removing a sealed packet. "Here. This is an eyepatch. It should help the detachment from affecting your overall vision. Feel free to drop by and see me if you or your team have any medical issues."

Alissa stopped to say goodbye to Nathan and Chris before leaving sickbay. As she entered the waiting area, the corpsman who had led her to the recovery unit was talking to a young seaman. On noticing Alissa, he pointed in her direction.

"That's her."

"Excuse me, ma'am?" The young seaman turned to Alissa. "Are you Miss Madison?"

"I am."

"Warrant Officer Marlowe, ma'am. The captain would like to see you on the bridge."

"That sounds ominous."

"Nothing to be worried about. He wants to discuss with you your options for the future."

Alissa motioned to the hatch. "Lead the way."

Chapter Three

THE BRIDGE WAS a bustle of activity. The ten-member crew, responsible for the steering, navigation, and communications of the ship, performed their duties under the command of the officer of the deck, while the boatswain's mate ensured all bridge watch stations were manned. No one paid attention when Alissa and Marlowe entered.

Marlowe excused himself, crossed over to the captain, and announced her arrival. The captain dismissed the warrant officer and strode over to Alissa.

"I'm Captain Evans." He extended his hand.

"Alissa Madison." She shook it. His grip was firm but not domineering.

"It's a pleasure to finally meet you. Lieutenant Hoskins briefed me about what happened on Warren Island. It's a miracle anyone made it out."

"Believe it or not, I've been through worse."

"Sadly, I do believe it. I haven't seen any deaders in person, but the horror stories from survivors who pass through here are numbing." For a brief second, the captain's professional demeanor faded into a grimace. "How are you and the others getting along? Is there anything you need?"

"The crew has been great in providing for us. I hope we're not in the way."

"Not at all. Since the outbreak, our job has primarily been rescue operations."

Evans escorted Alissa to the port bridge wing. "I wanted to

discuss your plans. I've been ordered by the acting president to withdraw the *Iwo Jima* to the Gulf of Mexico and assist with rescue operations there."

"Aren't you needed up here?"

"No, ma'am. No military units exist within three hundred miles of the east coast. As far as we can tell, you're among the last group of survivors in the northeast. Every other group that wanted to be rescued has been evacuated from the mainland. We've had radio contact with other survivors in New England and New York, but they all prefer to hunker down where they are and ride out the crisis. I assume there are others who refuse to contact us because they don't trust the military or the government. Because of that, the acting president feels we can be more useful down south where rescue operations are still proceeding. I have the authority to extract your people from New Hampshire and bring them aboard ship or, if you prefer, return you to your cabin. The choice is yours."

"If we're evacuated, where would we go?"

"We're removing all civilians to the White Sands Missile Range in New Mexico. That's where the government now is. There are about ten thousand people there. I know it sounds dangerous, but it's safe. The range is thirty-two hundred square miles of unpopulated territory. The defenses are excellent and there's minimal deader activity. It's the safest location in North America."

"What happens if I opt to stay here and we need to bug out later?"

"There are units west of the Mississippi to assist survivors in making it to safety but, to be honest, they don't have the manpower or capability to enter the dead zone. They can only offer help once you get to within a few miles of them. And that's next to impossible."

"Why's that?"

"Half the deader population between the river and the east coast followed the flow of refugees west. There are millions of them along the east banks of the Mississippi, in some places a mile deep. Less than five percent of the survivors who have attempted to escape west ever made it, and those are only the ones we knew about. If you stay here in New England, your chances of getting out later are slim."

Alissa felt overwhelmed by the information. What three days ago seemed like the safest option now sounded more like a death sentence.

"Not that I'm trying to sway your decision, ma'am," said Evans. "If you decide to join the last evac to New Mexico, it'll be one of the most protected operations we've carried out. Dr. Carrington and his team are heading out west with the blood samples, so we're ensuring an extensive security detail accompanies them. You, and especially the children, will be well protected."

Alissa weighed her options. There were so many pros and cons to staying and evacuation. She could not sort through them all. But then, this was not a decision she could make on her own. "Can I discuss it with my people first?"

"Of course."

"How long do I have to decide?"

"My orders are to leave the area by sundown. That gives us enough time as long as you let me know in the next few hours."

"I'll let you know by noon." Alissa nodded. "Thank you."

"My pleasure. I assume you know how to get back to your quarters."

"No armed escort?"

The captain smiled. "Not for you and your people. After what you did on Warren Island, we consider you one of us now."

ALISSA SWUNG BY their quarters to get the others. Kiera had already headed to sickbay to check on Nathan and Chris.

Luckily, Rebecca and Patricia had remained behind. The three women asked if Susie would mind dog sitting Shithead for a little while, which excited the young girl, and then set off for sickbay.

Once the group was together, Alissa explained to them their options and passed along the information Captain Evans had provided, then opened the floor to discussion.

"What do you think we should do?" asked Kiera.

Alissa shook her head. "I don't want to sway anyone's decision. I'm hoping we can reach a unanimous decision."

"I'm for staying in New Hampshire," said Nathan.

"Why?" Alissa asked.

"You told me what happened to you in Boston, and I saw what happened when Nahant and Warren Island were overrun. No way do I want to be trapped on a military base with ten thousand people and have one of them get infected. I've been through that too many times."

"What are the chances of that happening?" asked Kiera. "According to Alissa, White Sands has put into place security and quarantine measures to prevent that."

Nathan turned to her, his tone questioning and condescending. "Do you really trust the military to prevent everyone who's infected from getting onto the compound? Only one person has to slip though for the virus to spread."

"He's right," added Rebecca. "Look what happened on the island when the nurse became infected by...." She stopped herself, not wanting to bring up a touchy subject.

"It's okay," said Nathan. "Kiera told me the outbreak on the island began after the nurse pricked herself with a needle she had used to take my blood. It only proves my point. The military took safety precautions with me knowing I was infected and still an outbreak occurred. It's not worth the risk. We're safer staying in New Hampshire."

"I have to disagree." Chris propped himself up in his hospital bed. "Yes, there's the risk of being caught up in an outbreak if something goes wrong, but at least at White Sands we'll have better defenses and will be able to hold off an outside attack better."

"I assume you're referring to the attack a week ago on the cabin?" asked Alissa.

Chris nodded.

"We stopped them," said Nathan.

Kiera huffed. "Barely."

"That's an understatement," added Chris. "That's the closest we've come to death since the outbreak began. You almost died in that attack. That's the reason we're here."

"Wait a minute," interrupted Alissa. "No personal attacks."

"I'm only stating a fact." Chris looked over at Nathan. "I'm not blaming you for this. All I'm saying is you'd be among the bodies on that funeral pyre if your blood didn't fight off the virus. It's too dangerous to stay at the cabin by ourselves."

"I agree," added Kiera. "I didn't think we were going to make it off that roof alive."

Nathan held up his hands to stop the arguing. "I understand what you're saying. Yes, there are risks staying at the cabin. It's a miracle I survived that bite. We all know we're living on borrowed time. I'm only thinking about what's safer for the group. There are too many risks if we go on the road. Our safest bet is to stay put. Besides, what are the chances of another horde of deaders stumbling upon us?"

Rebecca looked to the others. "Didn't anyone tell him about the stampede?"

Nathan's eyes narrowed. "Stampede?"

Chris shook his head.

"I thought Alissa did," said Kiera.

Alissa flushed with embarrassment. "It slipped my mind."

"What are you talking about?"

Alissa took a deep breath. "While taking you to Warren Island, we came across a pack of about three hundred and fifty—"

"Three hundred and fifty?" asked Nathan.

Kiera nodded.

"—that swarmed the Humvee. They knocked us off the road and overwhelmed us. We'd all be dead if the military hadn't shown up to save us."

Chris took over. "The point is, there are a lot of dangers out there we don't know about. It's suicide to sit around in the cabin and hope they don't find us first."

Kiera nodded in agreement.

Rebecca jumped in. "Chris, you said there are a lot of dangers out there. Don't we run the risk of facing those same dangers if we head west?"

"I guess we do." Chris thought a moment. "But at least we'll have better protection on our trip."

"Will we?" Rebecca turned her attention to Alissa. "How are we getting to New Mexico?"

Alissa had no answer. "Captain Evans never said. He just told me that Dr. Carrington and the blood samples would be heading out west so the trip would have substantial military support."

Rebecca frowned. "I was on the road for months before I ran into you. It's horrible out there. I don't want to go back."

"Let's vote," said Alissa, ending the discussion. "All in favor of staying put at the cabin?"

Nathan and Rebecca raised their hands.

"All in favor of heading to White Sands?"

Chris and Kiera responded.

Alissa focused her gaze on Patricia. "What about you?"

"I have no say in this," said Patricia.

"You're part of the group now, so you have a vote."

Patricia leaned back in her chair and held her hands in front of her. "I'm grateful you saved us from that island. I'll gladly go along with whatever the majority decides."

"It's a tie." Chris rolled his eyes. "Two to two."

"Alissa hasn't voted yet," said Kiera.

"What's your choice?" Nathan crossed his arms over his chest.

Alissa avoided the topic. "Not everyone has voted yet. We still have to ask Miriam and Steve."

MIRIAM AND STEVE were on the other end of the radio. They had sent Little Stevie and Colleen upstairs to play with Archer. Both kids realized it was so the adults could talk in private.

Alissa explained the situation in detail as presented by Captain Evans as well as the discussions in the recovery unit so they both had as much information as the others on which to base their decision. When finished, she asked Miriam and Steve what they thought.

"What did the others decide?" asked Miriam.

"More importantly," added Steve, "what do you think is the best option?"

"I don't want to let you know what the others said. I want you make your decision on what you think is best and not be swayed by the rest of the group. Everybody agreed to stay together no matter what, so we do what the majority feels is best."

Miriam chuckled. "If I know Kiera, she voted to go on another adventure."

"And you don't know how the military intends to get us to New Mexico?" asked Steve.

"Captain Evans didn't say. And he promises this journey will have extra protection to guard Dr. Carrington and the blood samples."

"And once the *Iwo Jima* leaves, we're on our own?"

"Yes. There's no military left north of New Jersey and Pennsylvania. There are other groups in the area like us. There is a large community not too far from us at Naples. We passed through it on the way to Maine."

"I don't like that," said Miriam. "If we join up with them it means someone else other than you will be in charge."

"And we've already encountered smart deaders and the horde of stampeding dead," added Steve. "God only knows what other monstrosities are out there."

A moment of silence passed before Miriam came back online. "After what happened here last week, my vote is to head to New Mexico where it's safer."

"I'm not sure it will be," said Steve. "I agree with Nathan and Rebecca. The more people we're with, the greater the chances of a deader outbreak. Despite all the disadvantages, we're safer here."

"So that's your decision? One to stay and one to go?"

Both responded yes.

"What's the final vote?" asked Miriam.

The poll was three to go to New Mexico and three to hunker down in the cabin, which left Alissa with the unenviable task of being the tie breaker. She had hoped the others would be unanimous in the decision.

Alissa had been weighing the options all day. The thought of leaving the cabin, and especially all the supplies Paul had stockpiled over the years, distressed her. From here on in, they would be under the military's command. Not that she distrusted the military, but she hated the idea of giving up control of the group. It also bothered her that she had no idea what other horrors could be lurking out there. Maybe even more some smart deaders. If those things were evolving, that didn't bode well for them. And she didn't have any idea whether more hordes of stampeding deaders were out there. She knew the group could not survive another attack on the cabin like the one that had happened last week.

Plus, there were medical concerns. Nathan was fortunate to have not been turned by the bite he received. But the infection would have killed him if not for the military having more powerful anti-biotics. Chris and Steve both had bad legs that needed to heal. And she had the three children to worry about. Any major illness among the group would be fatal.

However, the idea of going on a cross-country trek offered little appeal. Alissa understood the reasoning of those who wanted to stay put. The images of the western part of the country that Captain Evans described frightened her. She had been through enough horrifying road trips to avoid enduring another one, especially one that involved thousands of miles of travel.

Either decision was fraught with challenges. The problem was, she would not know whether she made the right choice until it was too late to change her mind. Once again, she had to decide what would be better for the group in the long run.

"Alissa?" asked Miriam. "Are you there?"

"I'm here."

"What's the decision?"

"We're heading to New Mexico."

Chapter Four

A LISSA STOOD INSIDE the island by the hatch to the flight deck waiting for the all-clear to board the helicopter. Captain Alwell's crew, who had rescued them yesterday from Warren Island, would be flying them to the cabin to retrieve the others and as many supplies as they could carry. A second Super Stallion would be going along with a six-man contingent of Marines to provide military support if necessary. It would be a simple operation, according to Alwell. In, out, and done.

Arrangements had already been made with Miriam and Steve. They were to fill a backpack for everyone containing two sets of spare clothes and underwear, toiletries, needed medications, and anything else required. An extra backpack would contain food, bowls, and a small bag of kitty litter for Archer. The couple were also to gather a main weapon, secondary weapon, and bladed weapon for each adult member of the team and all the ammo for those weapons. Everything else, including food, would be left behind.

Alissa looked forward to changing her underwear. She had been wearing the same bra and panties since leaving the cabin four days ago. The only new additions to her outfit were the light blue shirt, a USS *Iwo Jima* baseball cap one of the crew gave her, and the eyepatch provided by Dr. Harris, the latter of which she felt self-conscious about even though it helped her see better.

Alissa looked at her watch. Kiera was ten minutes late. She smiled, figuring the girl was "tending" to Chris.

A minute later, Kiera finally arrived. "Sorry. I got lost. This is one huge-ass ship. I don't know how the crew finds their way around it."

"Lots of experience."

Kiera stepped back and examined Alissa. "You look like a pirate. All you need now is a fancy hat with a plume and a parrot."

Alissa laughed. "I could see the mayhem now if I introduced a parrot to Archer and Shithead."

"Yeah but think of the dirty words I could teach it." Kiera became serious. "Thanks for letting me go. It'll be nice to see Little Stevie and my parents again."

"They'll be as happy to see you."

"I hope so."

Alissa gave Kiera her best "mom" look.

"Okay, they will." Kiera changed subjects. "I can't believe we're leaving the cabin behind and heading to New Mexico."

"In the long run, it'll be safer."

"I agree. Have you ever been to New Mexico?"

"No, but I was in Tucson, Arizona once."

"What was that like?"

"Mostly desert, and the weather was hot but not humid."

"That doesn't sound too bad." Kiera paused. "I've never been farther south than Boston."

"Well, we're all in for an adventure."

The hatch to the flight deck opened. Ensign Kerwin, Alwell's crew chief, stepped inside followed by a gust of freezing air. "We're ready for departure, ma'am. Are you ladies all set?"

"We are."

"Then follow me, please."

Kerwin led them to the Super Stallion that sat fifty feet from the island. He assisted them inside. Six other crewmen sat opposite them, each buckled in with their headsets on. Kerwin closed and secured the troop door then checked to make certain they were all strapped in. Alissa donned her headset as the crew chief told the pilot they were ready. A few minutes later, both helicopters were airborne.

They made land north of Portland. Alissa leaned to the side and peered out the window. The area beneath them was pristine with freshly fallen snow as far as they could see. It brought home to her how desolate New England had become. None of the roads had been plowed, not even I-95, the interstate highway that ran from Key West to the Canadian border. Nothing moved down below, at least nothing that could be seen. God knows how many deaders were buried under the snow. After being ambushed by and nearly overrun by them on Warren Island, Alissa was glad she would never find out.

Kiera reached over and tapped Alissa's shoulder to get her attention, mouthing the words, "This is awesome."

Alissa smiled and gave her a thumbs up. She couldn't blame Kiera for being excited. That was the part of the fun of being a teenager. Alissa, on the other hand, had more than her share of such rides. She had been aboard three choppers in as many days and, each time, the circumstances had not been ideal. This ride was no exception.

After nearly thirty minutes, they passed over North Conway. The city appeared serene. All traces of their last encounter had been erased, three feet of snow burying the carcasses of hundreds of deaders and charred buildings as well as camouflaging in white the thousands of acres of burnt forests.

Alwell's voice came over the headset. "Miss Madison, could you come to the cockpit?"

"Be right there." Alissa made her way forward to join the pilot, tapping him on the shoulder to let him know she had arrived. "You wanted to see me?"

"Yes, ma'am. I need you to direct me to your cabin."

Alissa looked out the cockpit windshield, familiarizing herself with the surroundings. She had visited North Conway scores of times over the years, but never from the air. After a few minutes, she got her bearings and pointed to Route 302 off in the distance.

"Follow that road north. My cabin is along there."

Alwell veered the Super Stallion so it followed the road. A few minutes later, Alissa spotted her cabin along the ridge.

"There it is."

"Thank you, ma'am. You better go back and strap in."

As Alissa complied, Alwell brought the Super Stallion in over the compound. There was no place to set down near the cabin, the only suitable area being the main road at the end of the driveway. Even that would be tight, but doable.

"Sky Queen One to Sky Queen Two, do you read me? Over."

"Sky Queen Two to Sky Queen One, read you loud and clear. Over."

"We've reached our objective, Sky Queen Two. I'm going to set down on the road, but first I want to do some plowing. Stay close and be ready to provide support if needed. Roger that? Over."

"Roger that, Sky Queen One. Call us if you need us. Over and out."

Alwell positioned the helicopter over the compound and descended to an altitude of one hundred and fifty feet, hovering above the tree line. The backwash from the blades churned up the snow in the cabin's front yard, blowing it to the sides. He slowly maneuvered the Super Stallion down the driveway, using the backwash to clear away the snow, before finally landing on the two-lane road. He shut down the engines. The rotors slowed and churned to a stop. As Kerwin slid aside the port troop door, those in the cabin removed their headsets, jumped out, and readied their weapons for combat. Alissa and Kiera exited last and led the others up the driveway.

The gate blocking the driveway was closed and locked. Despite the backwash from the helicopter, considerable snow remained piled on either side of the gate and chain link fence.

Sergeant Harrigan, the leader of the military unit, used the stock of his M4 to bust open the lock. The six of them grabbed the right side of the gate and shoved it open enough for them to pass through. They proceeded up to the cabin.

Miriam and the others stood on the porch waiting for them. Kiera broke from the group and raced ahead to greet her mother. Miriam and Little Stevie met her halfway across the front yard. The three embraced.

Miriam held Kiera tight, wrapping one hand around her head and pulling her close. "I'm so glad to see you. I was worried sick about you."

"I love you, mom."

Miriam squeezed Kiera and began crying.

"I'm okay, mom. I promise."

"I want a hug, too," protested Little Stevie.

Kiera broke free from her mother, crouched, and hugged her brother. After a minute, she broke the hug, reached into her shirt pocket, and removed the Spiderman figurine. "Look what I still have. It kept me safe the entire time."

"Did you kill any deaders while you were gone?" he asked.

"Lots of them. And I got to fire a machine gun."

"Awesome! Tell me about it."

Harrigan interrupted them. "I hate to break up this family reunion, but we need to load the chopper and get back to the ship ASAP."

"I understand," said Miriam. "There's several duffle bags in the living room. Do you need help with them?"

"We're fine, ma'am. Thank you." Harrigan turned to his unit and told them to bring the duffle bags back to the helicopter.

Alissa and the others followed. "What did you bring?"

"The only weapons left were the Mk 14 Enhanced Battle Rifle with the sniper scope, the two 10mm Smith and Wesson revolvers, and the two Colt .45s. Archer is in his carrier on the dining room table. He's not happy."

Alissa chuckled. "He's going to be really unhappy on the ride to the ship."

Steve waved from the front porch. "Glad you all made it back safe."

Kiera hugged him. "I love you."

He fought back his tears. "I love you, too, kid."

Kiera didn't break the hug but sighed. "I'm not a kid anymore."

"You'll always be my kid to me."

Connie greeted Alissa. "Is Aunt Rebecca okay?"

"She's fine, honey. She's waiting for you on the ship."

"Good."

"And we have another girl joining our group. Susie. She lost her parents like you did, so I want you to be nice to her."

"Really?"

Alissa nodded.

"Yay. I have a sister as well as a brother."

Little Stevie playfully rolled his eyes at the prospect of having another sister.

The military exited the cabin, four of them carrying duffle bags while Harrigan and another soldier stayed on either side of them, guns at the ready in case any deaders appeared.

"We have one more trip," said the sergeant. "Then we're out of here."

"Let me get Archer. The rest of you, grab the overnight bags and help get Steve down to the chopper."

"We're riding in a helicopter?" asked Little Stevie.

"Yes."

"Pissah."

Alissa heard Archer's protests from the front porch. She stepped over to the carrier and called his name. The whining stopped. On seeing his mistress, the cat meowed. Alissa opened the carrier door, reached in, and pulled him out. Archer snuggled against her chest, purring contentedly as he ran his head across her face.

"I missed you so much," she whispered.

Archer licked her nose.

The protesting began again when she placed him back in the carrier and secured the door. Picking up the carrier and the overnight back with cat supplies, she exited onto the porch.

Kiera helped her father down the driveway with Little Stevie and Connie right behind them. Miriam waited for her.

"I hate to leave this place," she said. "Despite the attack last week."

"I do, too. But it's for the best."

"I hope so." Miriam did not sound convinced. "What will happen to it?"

"The military have the geocoordinates for its location. If they contact someone who needs a place to stay, they'll direct them here."

"So, it'll still be of use."

"Hopefully." Alissa stared at the cabin. This place had saved their lives. Was she putting them in harm's way by leaving it? For a moment, she wondered if she had made the correct decision. Then her eyes fell upon the snow-covered funeral pyre of the hundreds of smart deaders that had attacked them a week ago, convincing her she was right.

The military returned to retrieve the last of the duffle bags. As they exited, Harrigan stepped over to the two women. "Sorry, ma'am. We need to get going."

"I understand."

The women fell in behind the military. Archer whined the entire time. When they reached the Super Stallion, the military stowed the last of the gear. Alissa and Miriam climbed on board. Kerwin made certain the civilians were buckled in and wearing their headsets. Little Stevie sat by the window on the starboard side, excited for the upcoming ride. Kiera sat beside him, telling him how much fun it would be. The others sat across from them, Steve holding Connie's hand. Alissa and Miriam took seats by the port door.

When everything was secure, Kerwin slid shut the troop door, buckled himself in, and announced they were ready. Alwell started the engines. When they reached full power, he lifted the Super Stallion off the road, ascending to a safe flight level.

Alissa glanced out the window at her cabin several hundred feet below. A part of her felt a terrible sense of loss. For better or worse, she was leaving behind a major part of her life. A life she and Paul had built together. A life of survival under apocalyptic circumstances. A life where she had surprised herself with her own courage and versatility. A life where, despite the losses among their group, she had probably saved the lives of several people who would otherwise be dead now.

Alissa hoped the new life she had chosen for herself and the group would be one as positive.

Chapter Five

THE CONVOY THUNDERED north along I-25. Two tractor trailers filled with what was taken from the train. A school bus carrying the Scavengers who launched the attack. And Slade in the lead driving the Hummer H3, with Gina up front and Mauler and another bodyguard in back. Desert stretched on either side as far as the horizon, which suited Slade perfectly. No deaders could descend upon them without being spotted well in advance, nor could any of the settlements they had attacked launch an ambush against them.

The haul from this morning's raid had been acceptable. They had confiscated enough MREs to feed the group for a week and enough medical supplies to finally shut up Doc and keep everyone healthy enough to work. New clothes would be welcomed by the workers, many of whom still wore what the same outfits they had when the outbreak occurred. Big Jake would be pleased with the three new editions to the brothel. The guys would pay big for a chance at some fresh pussy.

Most important of all, they had blocked the rail line to Albuquerque. From now on, the military would have to use land routes to supply White Sands, which made Slade's job that much easier.

The convoy passed a road sign that read:

Pueblo   10 miles
Colorado Springs   54 miles
Denver   125 miles

Almost home, thought Slade.

Home was an armed compound he had set up a few miles south of Pueblo. Most of the idiots who had survived the outbreak had sought shelter in what they thought were secure areas to ride out the apocalypse, if you could call super stores, warehouses, and National Guard barracks secure. Some assholes hunkered down in their own homes, thinking a thousand rounds of ammo and a month's supply of food would save them. It might have if it had been a natural disaster or social unrest. But not against a full-fledged fucking deader apocalypse. Those few groups that survived the hordes soon had to contend with lack of food and water, most being overrun minutes after leaving their secured areas.

Slade did the exact opposite. He found the ideal location to ride out the end of the world then fortified it. It included the Saint Charles Reservoirs Number Two and Three to the west of I-25 and the Vestas wind turbine factory across the highway. Once he had an unlimited source of water and power, he began pulling together a team to fortify the location and gather supplies from local supermarkets. The reservoirs didn't need to be protected because deaders avoided water. Rather than construct an impenetrable defense around the turbine complex, they reinforced the chain link fence that already existed around the compound by circling it with the abandoned vehicles from the compound and the highway. Morning and late afternoon patrols roamed the perimeter, putting down any deaders that tried to get in. Those numbers significantly dropped two months ago when Zach, his tech guru, set up a mobile radio station ten miles to the west in the desert. The music played constantly, attracting deaders away from the compound and out into the middle of nowhere to roast in the sun. Zach had installed a camera on the makeshift radio tower to monitor his progress. At last count, several thousand deaders milled around the radio station.

The convoy reached the twin reservoirs. Slade slowed and

took the exit ramp, turning right onto Little Road and following it to Tower Road. The wind turbine complex loomed before them. The factory itself, several hundred acres in area, served as the warehouse, motor pool, and living quarters for the single workers who lived there. Families, what few there were, lived in the offices on the first floor of the admin building. The compound's security force and raiders occupied the second floor, Zach and other key people the third floor, the bodyguard unit the fourth, and Slade the fifth. The smaller of the two factories had been converted into the brothel where Slade allowed his people to blow off steam any way they wanted. Last was the motor pool, which had been converted into The Pit.

As the convoy pulled into the center of the compound, the two trucks broke off and headed for the warehouse to unload. Slade led the rest to the admin building, parking out front. The school bus rolled up beside him and stopped. Tony stepped over, greeting the Boss as he climbed out of the Hummer.

"I'm going to head over to the warehouse and make sure the medical supplies we picked up get sent over to Doc."

"Good idea," said Slade. "And make it clear to him this was all we could find and I don't want to hear any more of his bitching."

"With pleasure."

"I'm also telling Big Jake that you and the other raiders have an open tab tonight. You earned it."

"Thanks, Boss."

The rest of the Scavengers got off the bus bringing with them two of the women they had kidnapped. The younger of the two, barely in her early twenties, appeared terrified, her eyes wide open and examining everything, like a frightened rabbit in an uncertain situation. The older woman, who seemed closer to thirty, had lost her spirit. She followed the others off the bus, her eyes focused on the ground, obeying what her captors told her to do without responding.

Neither was the case with the bitch from the engine. She still had a lot of fight in her. It took two Scavengers to drag her off the bus, the bitch resisting the entire time. Once on the ground, she kicked her two guards in the ankles.

"Let me go, motherfuckers."

Mauler went over to straighten her out. He stood in front of her, towering above the woman.

"If I were you, bitch, I'd settle down."

She became docile.

"Do you want me to bring her to the brothel?" asked Tony.

"Fuck no. I don't need one of the guys getting his dick bit off."

"I'll smack her into shape," said Gina.

"No." Slade glared at Gina, letting her know she had stepped out of line, then turned his attention to Tony. "Lock her in one of the cells. Devon said he needs help at The Pit. Take her over there tonight. A few weeks there should knock the feistiness out of here."

"Yes, Boss."

As the others went about their business, Slade glanced over at Gina.

"I'm sorry," she mumbled.

He pinched her ass hard. "You'll make it up to me. I want to celebrate our success."

"Anything for you."

Slade smiled. He planned on taking her up on that.

Chapter Six

THE LAST SIXTEEN hours aboard the *Iwo Jima* were quite pleasant despite the reality that Alissa's group were refugees aboard an American naval vessel. Everyone was glad to be together again. Shithead got the most attention, mostly from Little Stevie and Connie who showered him with affection. Along with Susie, the children conspired to sneak Shithead into sick bay to see Chris, a breach of the rules that Dr. Harris allowed until the dog jumped into bed with its master.

Despite the incident, Harris agreed to provide each member of the group a physical before they set off across the country. Everyone checked out fine with two minor exceptions. The doctor told Steve he needed to use his leg more so it wouldn't atrophy, a recommendation Miriam mercilessly teased him about. And Alissa had a blood pressure reading slightly above the norm, which was natural considering the stress she had been under the past week.

That night they all slept well knowing they were together and safe from any external threats.

At 0700 the next morning, they gathered in the area inside the island, waiting for the Super Stallion to be readied to take them to St. Louis. Woody and Ben, the two snowplow drivers who had saved them on Warren Island, were also taking the flight out. Alwell would be flying them to their destination and would reconnect with the *Iwo Jima* later in the Gulf of Mexico. Dr. Carrington and his only assistant, a young man named

Kevin who had survived the deader outbreak on Warren Island, patiently waited by the hatch, the ice pack containing the blood samples they had obtained from Boston at his feet in a cooler. The kids were excited about having another ride in a helicopter and chatted amongst themselves. The more they talked, the more nervous Rebecca became. She finally walked away and joined Alissa.

"Are you okay?" asked Alissa. "You look pale."

"Is it that obvious?"

"Yes, but I'm a nurse."

Rebecca chuckled. "I'm terrified of flying. Joel and I once flew to Vegas for a weekend. I crushed his hand the entire time."

"You can hold mine if you want to."

"I might take you up on that. Listening to the kids relate their experiences made me even more upset. I hated yesterday's flight, and that was only half an hour. The idea of flying halfway across the country where I can see everything on the ground scares me."

"Don't worry," Alissa tried to reassure her. "I've flown with Alwell before. He's a good pilot."

"Not as good as me." The familiar voice of Sam Robson, the pilot who had flown them into Boston and saved them on Warren Island, came from behind Alissa.

"How sweet. You came to wish us luck."

"Yes. And to ask a favor."

"Anything. I wouldn't be here if not for you."

Robson smiled and pulled an envelope from inside his inner jacket pocket which he handed to Alissa. The name Stephanie Clark was written on it. "My fiancée is stationed at White Sands. When you get there, could you make sure she gets this?"

"Of course."

"I haven't talked to her in over a month. I'm sure she's worried."

"It's my pleasure. And I promise not to tell her about all the close calls we had together."

"Thank you. She'd kill me if she knew the chances I've been taking."

Alissa slid the envelope into the inner pocket of her letter jacket then hugged Robson. "Thank you for everything."

"Thank you." He hugged her tight. When he was finished, he saluted Alissa. "Godspeed on your trip. May the wind always be at your back."

As Robson walked off, Chris limped over. "Looks like you have yourself quite a harem."

The look Alissa flashed him was colder than the weather outside.

Kerwin opened the hatch leading to the flight deck and leaned in, accompanied by a blast of cold air. "Your gear is loaded. We're ready for you."

One at a time, Alissa's team made their way to the helicopter and took their seats. The kids each got a window seat. Rebecca saved one beside her for Alissa. Once everyone was aboard, the crew chief slid shut the troop door and made certain everyone was strapped in.

Five minutes later, the Super Stallion lifted off the flight deck and headed west toward the United States.

THE SUPER STALLION made landfall near Point Pleasant Beach on New Jersey. Alwell kept the helicopter at an altitude of five thousand feet. The nor'easter that nearly got so many of them killed had not touched this part of the country, so everything below them was clear. Stray deaders wandered the back roads and countryside. Other than that, the area appeared serene, showing no indication that an apocalypse had nearly destroyed all life on the planet.

That changed when the helicopter flew over I-95, the interstate that ran the length of the east coast. Bumper-to-bumper traffic filled the highway, creating a gridlock that had been a death sentence for anyone attempting to escape that way. Thousands of deaders staggered between the abandoned vehicles, bumping into each other. Everyone imagined what a nightmare it must have been to be trapped inside their cars when the deaders fell upon them. Even the kids, who had been excited by the trip, looked away and became somber. Alissa wondered how many survived the attacks and what had happened to them since.

A few minutes later, they flew north of Philadelphia. The city had been ravaged by the outbreak, much more than Boston. A residential neighborhood in the suburbs to the south had burnt to the ground. Three skyscrapers within the city limits were gutted by uncontrolled fires, their burnt hulks clearly visible even at this distance. Like I-95, all the roads leading out of Philadelphia were jammed with abandoned vehicles with thousands of deaders intermingled among them.

Alissa's stomach sickened as she experienced flashbacks of her own nightmare in Boston that first day. Unable to take anymore, she leaned her head back against the bulkhead and took a nap.

ALWELL'S VOICE COMING through the headset woke Alissa.

"Refueling Station Charlie, this is Sky Queen One. Do you copy? Over."

"Sky Queen One, this is Refueling Station Charlie. We read you loud and clear. Over."

"We're about twenty minutes out. Are you ready to receive us? Over."

"Affirmative, Sky Queen One. The area is secure. We'll have the welcome wagon waiting for you. Over and out."

Alissa keyed her microphone. "We're at St. Louis already?"

"No, ma'am," replied Alwell. "We don't have the fuel range to make it to St. Louis in one flight, so we're gassing up at one of the refueling stations set up by the military."

"Is it safe?"

"Yes, ma'am. These guys know what they're doing. It's one of the safest locations in the dead zone."

They flew past the landscape for several miles. The ground below was desolate with no sign of living dead activity. After several minutes, Alissa failed to spot a single deader. She was about to question it when Alwell's voice came over the headset.

"Refueling Station Charlie, we have visual. Request permission to land. Over."

"Permission granted. I hope you were able to procure the necessary supplies. Over."

"I always take care of you, good buddy."

The Super Stallion approached a state penitentiary surrounded by cement walls. The courtyard had been cleared of benches and exercise equipment and now served as a landing pad. Hundreds of fifty-five-gallon drums of gasoline lined the prison walls. Five soldiers stood by the wall waiting. Only one carried an M4. A sixth stood in the center of the pad guiding in the helicopter. Alwell maneuvered it over the area. The soldier gave him the signal to land and rushed to join the others. Alwell brought down the Super Stallion to a soft landing then turned off the engines.

"We need to have the chopper empty during refueling. Get out, stretch your legs, and use the head if you need to. We'll be airborne again in about thirty minutes."

One of the soldiers by the wall came over and slid open the starboard troop door. He was tall, with tanned skin and sported a think black beard as if he had just returned from a tour to the Middle East. He had an unusual glare in his brown eyes. Not PTSD and not quite insanity. He reminded Alissa of the Tom Hank's character from *Castaway*.

"I'm Lieutenant Andrews. Welcome to the eighth circle of

Hell. If you need to take a leak, you can do so around the corner. If you need privacy, Sergeant Stephenson will show you to the latrines."

Another tall man with a red beard and long hair nodded. The women and Dr. Carrington, the latter carrying the cooler, followed the sergeant inside the prison. Nathan, Chris, Woody, Ben, and the two Steves headed around the building. Shithead did his business twenty feet from the helicopter.

Alissa hung around to watch as the remaining soldiers rolled over drums of gasoline and began the refueling process.

"Where are we?" she asked.

"The Southern Ohio Correctional Institute. About fifty miles east of Cincinnati. It's the ideal location for a refueling station. The walls keep the deaders out. And no one in his right mind wants to leave."

In the distance Alissa heard a distinct, continuous wail. It sounded as if it was all around them.

"What's that noise?"

"Air raid sirens, ma'am. We set up a pair in the rivers west and south of us. It draws the deaders away from us and they get washed away. We have another one located inside a Super Walmart to the east. Got hundreds of the bastards trapped in there. I wish we could call an airstrike on the place and get rid of them."

"Creative."

"Thanks. We remotely set them off for an hour every three days or when a chopper is flying in. We haven't seen any of those dead motherfucker things in weeks."

"How long have you been here?" Alissa asked.

"Five weeks now. One more week and we get switched out for another crew of unlucky bastards who'll do their six weeks. Not soon enough, if you ask me."

Alissa watched the refueling process. As one member of each two-man team placed the end of a long hose into the Super Stallion's gas tank, the second inserted the other end into the drum and used an electric pump to transfer the gasoline. Shithead wandered over to say hello. One of the soldiers, a young woman with her blonde hair in a ponytail, crouched down to pet him, receiving a face bath. She laughed and scratched behind the dog's ears. The fun ended when the corporal filling the tank snapped at her to keep her mind on her work. She gave Shithead one final scratch behind his ears, kissed him on the forehead, and sent him on his way.

One by one, the others filtered back to the landing area. Miriam walked over to Alissa, a sour expression on her face.

"Everything okay?" asked Alissa.

"The toilets are disgusting. I think the Army teaches the men that as long as they hit something they're doing well."

Alissa laughed, the first time she had done so in God knows when.

Forty minutes later, the tight-assed corporal removed the hose from the helicopter and replaced the fuel cap. "All set."

Alwell leaned over to Andrews. "Isn't he going to clean the windshield?"

"That'll be $600."

"Do you take credit cards?"

"Fuck no."

"How about a trade?" Alwell walked over the main cabin. Kerwin jumped in ahead of him and passed out eleven boxes, ten cases of Corona beer and one of Jack Daniels. "Will that do?"

Bellemah broke open the case of whiskey, pulled out a bottle, unscrewed the cap, and took a long swig. When finished, the lieutenant smacked his lips loudly.

"For this, I'd let you date my daughter, if I had one. Do you need anything else?"

"Just clear sailing to St. Louis."

"I wish I could help with that." Andrews shook Alwell's hand. "Good luck."

"Same to you." Alwell stepped back and yelled out, "All

right, people. Everybody back on board. We have a schedule to keep."

Not long after, the Super Stallion lifted off from Refueling Station Charlie and headed west.

ALISSA HAD FALLEN asleep on the second leg of the flight. She had no idea for how long. Two things woke her up – a nervous Rebecca squeezing her hand and light from a setting sun streaming through the windshield. She pulled the *Iwo Jima* baseball cap down to shade her eyes. It blocked the light, but she could not fall back to sleep. Instead. she sat there, trying to relax and not think about what lay ahead.

A few minutes later, Alwell's voice came over the headset. "We're about to pass over the Mississippi River. St. Louis is off to starboard. Check it out if you want to see something really horrifying."

Alissa, Nathan, and Chris unbuckled their belts and moved to the starboard window. Alissa peered out and wished she hadn't.

The six bridges leading from Illinois into St. Louis had been destroyed, the remnants of their center spans dangling above the river. Only a controlled detonation could have done that type of damage. Alissa knew that. She had barely survived such an incident while escaping from Boston. Hundreds of abandoned vehicles filled the eastern approaches to the bridges. The front tires of a few closest to the collapse dangled precariously off the destroyed roads. Even more stretched along the roads on the eastern side of the Mississippi leading into the city, gridlocked like every major highway on the country and turned into a feeding ground for the living dead.

Even more disturbing, the east bank of the river swarmed with living dead, stretching north and south to the horizons. Swarm was an understatement. Deaders lined the shore for miles, fifty to one hundred in depth, forming a gigantic mob of the living dead that pushed and shoved against the riverbank. Unlike previous hordes of deaders, this one did not rush into the water like lemmings off a cliff, wiping out their numbers en masse. These deaders paused at the water's edge. Occasionally one would drop off the jagged edge of a blown bridge or be pushed into the river, the bodies being swept away in the current. The mass stared across the river as if waiting for someone to ferry them across. Alissa shivered from the cold chill that crept down her spine.

"What are they doing?" asked Nathan.

Alissa shook her head. "I have no idea."

"They've been doing that for the past few weeks," explained Alwell over the headset. "At first, those damns things charged into the Mississippi to get to those of us on the other side. Tens of thousands were washed away. About a month ago they stopped that behavior, almost as if they realized what would happen to them. Now they keep on piling up along the bank."

"Sentience," whispered Chris.

"I didn't catch that," said Alwell.

"Smart deaders. We ran into some back in New Hampshire."

"Are you telling me these fucking these are becoming intelligent?" asked Canderossi, the co-pilot.

"Not intelligent like us," explained Chris. "The ones we ran into had developed the ability to hunt in packs and ambush their prey."

Canderossi shook his head. "We can't catch a fucking break."

"I wonder how many are down there?" asked Alissa.

"Intel estimates twenty to thirty million between Minneapolis and New Orleans," said Alwell. "Most followed the survivors as they evacuated to the west. That's why all bridges across the river were destroyed."

"God," said Nathan. "I would hate to have been the officer who had to give that order."

"He committed suicide less than twenty-four hours after issuing it." Alwell paused. "If you could take your seats. I'm making the final approach to our destination."

Alissa and the others sat down and buckled in.

Not long after, Alwell called their destination.

"Oregon Trail Prime, this is Sky Queen One. Do you copy? Over."

Silence.

"Oregon Trail Prime, this is Sky Queen One. Do you copy? Over."

A female voice with a New York accent responded. "We read you loud and clear, Sky Queen One. We're prepared for your arrival. Over."

"Thank you, Oregon Trail Prime. We'll be touching down in approximately ten minutes."

The Super Stallion began a slow descent. Alissa sat up in her seat and stretched to look out the windshield.

A few miles ahead of them sat an industrial facility composed of three large and two medium-sized buildings covering two hundred acres of land. A wall of shipping containers formed a square around the perimeter stacked two high. Five strands of barbed wire extended horizontally around the outer edges, held in place by metal rods welded to the containers. Alissa had seen this before at the ferry terminal leading to Warren Island. Though effective, it was a backstop to the primary defense. A trench twenty feet deep and ten feet wide sat two hundred yards from the wall and circled the compound. Three flamethrower teams, each guarded by ten armed soldiers, walked the interior side of the trench, incinerating any deaders trapped inside. A backhoe followed each team scooping out the ashes and dumping them on the exterior side. The mound of ashes on the other side testified to how many deaders had unsuccessfully attacked the compound.

"Sky Queen One, this is Oregon Trail Prime. You are cleared for landing. Over."

"Roger that. Thanks, Over."

The Super Stallion landed in a clearing between the buildings where a makeshift landing pad had been painted onto the cement. Ten civilians waited near the pad. Once the blades ground to a halt, they ran over. Kerwin opened the troop doors.

The leader of the group, a tall man of average looks, with close cropped blonde hair and piercing blue eyes, centered himself in the opening. "Welcome to Oregon Trail Prime, twenty miles west of St. Louis. I'm Travis Whitaker. I'm in charge of this complex. My team here will take your gear and load them onto tomorrow's train. I'm here to show you around."

As everyone climbed out, Rebecca pausing to look to the heavens and thanking God for getting them here safely, Alissa stepped over to the pilot's door and knocked. Alwell opened it.

"Can I help you, ma'am?"

Alissa extended her hand. "I wanted to say thanks for everything you've done for us. We'd be stranded in Maine if not for you and your crew."

Alwell took her hand and gave it a firm but friendly shake. "Just doing my job." The smile told her he appreciated the gesture.

Alissa joined the others.

"We're nowhere near Oregon," said Patricia. "Why do you call this place Oregon Trail Prime?"

"Did you ever play video games?" asked Ben.

"No."

"Let's just say it's a sick joke."

"It's more then a sick joke," explained Whitaker. "It's a reminder that no matter how safe we are here, the trip to White Sands is still dangerous. There are a lot of deaders between here and Alamogordo."

"The crew of the *Iwo Jima* said you've never lost anyone."

Whitaker's pleasant demeanor faded. "That was true until yesterday. We lost a supply train to Scavengers. The crew of thirteen were killed or taken prisoner, and everything those assholes didn't take with them they burned."

"What are Scavengers?" asked Woody.

"They're a group of bandits from Colorado who run their turf like it's a fiefdom. The leader of the group is a crazy son of a bitch named Slade. They left us alone for the first few months following the outbreak, but lately they've been encroaching on our territory, launching raids into northern New Mexico. Yesterday they ambushed one of our supply trains."

The general joviality of the group suddenly turned sour.

"So how are we going to get to White Sands?" asked Alissa.

"We have you covered on that. We'll brief you on all the details in the morning." Whitaker stepped away from the group. "If you'll follow me, I'll show you where you can bunk down for the night."

"How many people live here now?" asked Miriam.

"Only a thousand, but they're all workers. When it was a refugee camp, it held close to twenty thousand."

"Damn," muttered Nathan. "How did you fit them all in here?"

"Barely. When the new government established itself at White Sands, most of the military and civilians moved out west to be safer."

"Why didn't you go with them?"

"Several reasons. We wanted to keep this as a safe zone for those evacuating from the east who were lucky enough to get across the Mississippi. The only other safe zone like this is outside Rapid City, South Dakota. When our numbers started growing in the first weeks of the outbreak, we set up our own facilities to keep the people alive. The military brought in truckloads of MREs to feed us and we began a major operation to distill hundreds of gallons of water a day."

"Where did you get the water?" asked Alissa.

"A unit from the Army Corps of Engineers ran a pipeline from the Mississippi River to here. They lost a lot of men doing it but, without that pipeline, we would have been screwed. The military sent out massive raiding parties that gathered tons of weapons, food, and clothing for the population. We were lucky that the office complex," Whitaker pointed to the building where they were heading, "had a doc-in-the-box and a food shelter. We set up a team that started producing medicines from scratch, mostly herbal, but they worked. None of these facilities have been established yet at White Sands so we agreed to stay behind and provide supplies for the new government until they were self-sufficient. Once they are, most of us will move to New Mexico."

They reached the office complex. Whitaker led them inside and up to the sixth floor. The offices had been taken over for living spaces, with all the furniture neatly piled against one wall, the open floor rest containing sleeping bags and the personal belongings of the crew. He led them to an office at the far end of the hall that held two dozen sleeping bags. Whitaker ushered them inside.

"This is the guest room. All the sleeping bags have been washed. Make yourselves at home. We're keeping the mess hall open until seven so you can eat. Let me know if you need anything."

Carrington stepped forward and held up the cooler. "Do you have a place where I can store these?"

"Are those the blood samples that hold the possible vaccine?"

"They are."

"Follow me. I'll take you the clinic. They can store them there. They'll prep them in the morning for the run to White Sands."

"Thank you."

Whitaker turned to the others. "I'll see you all tomorrow

morning at 0700 for the briefing. Good night."

When Whitaker and Carrington left, the others claimed sleeping bags as their own. "Should we head down to supper before they close the cafeteria?" asked Nathan.

"You guys go ahead." Alissa grabbed the end of one of the blankets and pulled it over to the window. She placed the carrier and travel bag with cat supplies on the floor. "I need to change his litter box first."

"That's a good enough reason for me to leave," joked Steve.

"I'll join you in a few minutes."

When everyone had left, Alissa opened the door to the carrier. Archer sat in the rear of the carrier in his litter box, not at all happy with his treatment over the past twenty-four hours. He glared at Alissa and meowed angrily.

"Stop being a dick."

Archer paused for a second then issued a short, deep meow. Alissa reached in and pulled the litter box toward the opening. He jumped out, ran over to the other side of the room, and groomed himself. Alissa cleaned out the soiled sections of the box and poured in some fresh litter. She then removed his two dishes, a can of cat food, and a bottle of water and made his dinner. The idea of a meal enticed Archer, who returned and rubbed against Alissa's arm before eating.

Alissa threw the bag of used litter in the trash can in the bathroom, washed her hands, and joined the others for dinner.

Chapter Seven

AFTER DINNER, CHRIS took Shithead on a walk around the compound. After being separated from him for so long, it was nice to have time to reconnect. The dog stayed beside him the entire time, every few minutes making eye contact with his master with that look of adoration only a dog can feel for its human. The night was cool, Chris guessing the temp to be in the low fifties, which seemed balmy considering the freeze New England had been going through. He kept his jacket unzipped, enjoying the weather as they circled the compound before heading back to their quarters.

Shithead broke away from Chris and raced ahead. Nathan sat on a picnic table outside the office complex that the crew used as a smoking station. His back was to them. Shithead barked once as he bounded across the open space. Nathan shifted in his seat and smiled.

"Come on, boy."

Shithead reached the table, jumped onto the bench beside Nathan, and gave him a face bath.

Chris joined them, sitting on the table with his feet on the bench. "Getting some air, Patient Zero?"

Nathan rolled his eyes. "I hate that name. It sounds like I'm the cause of all this."

"You might be the cure."

"That's a lot of responsibility. I'm not sure if I'm up to it."

"It's not like you have to do anything other than give them your blood and let the scientists do the rest."

"I know." Nathan hesitated. "Because of me, you, Alissa, and Kiera almost got killed taking me to Warren Island."

"You guys would have done the same for me."

"Probably. Then your trip back into Boston."

"Don't remind me." Chris unconsciously rubbed the wound on his leg. "But that had nothing to do with you."

"I caused the outbreak on Warren Island that got everyone killed."

"That was not your fault. The nurse pricked herself with the needle she used to draw your blood."

"I'm infected," said Nathan with a hint of despair in his tone.

"Not anymore. You fought it off, which means your blood can be the cure for all this. And we wouldn't have known that without taking you to Maine."

"I guess."

An awkward silence passed between the two men.

Nathan spoke first. "Can I ask you something?"

"Sure."

"You like Alissa, don't you?"

"Is it that obvious?"

Nathan nodded. "Do you feel the same way toward her?"

"Yes."

"I thought so. And it's obvious she cares for you."

"She also likes you."

"I know." Nathan searched for the right words. "Have you two... been together?"

Chris said nothing.

"I thought so." Nathan had a tone of dejection in his voice.

"Is that going to be an issue between us? I don't want to ruin our friendship."

"It's okay. I can't hold it against either of you. Of all our concerns, that one is pretty low on the list."

"I can back out if you want?"

"You mean leave the group?" asked Nathan.

"I mean take myself out of the romantic picture."

"That's up for Alissa to decide. You're a valuable member of the group. Besides, I enjoy having you as a friend."

"Thanks." Chris patted Nathan on the shoulder. "Same here."

"Everything is cool between us?"

"It always has been."

Nathan smiled. "I'm glad that's out in the open and settled."

"Who knows." Chris nudged his friend. "Maybe we can get a three-way out of it."

Nathan laughed. "I always hoped if that happened it would be me and two girls."

Chris smiled and winked.

"Bullshit."

"It happened one weekend in Vegas."

"So you paid for it."

"What happens in Vegas stays in Vegas."

Both men got a much-needed chuckle. After a few more minutes of idle talk, they went inside to bunk down for the night.

Chapter Eight

MONICA HAD BEEN escorted at gunpoint by five Scavengers across the compound to a large building with three large sliding doors that had once served as the maintenance garage. Tony opened the entrance to the office and entered.

The office itself was sparsely decorated. An old, banged up metal desk and chair with the seat and back cushions worn down stood by the door. A laptop sat open on it. A gun stand stood against one wall containing five various semi-automatic weapons, a chain running through the trigger guards of each weapon and anchored to the ends with padlocks. A scuffed metal filing cabinet stood to its right. An old calendar from last year hung on the wall. It was turned to November. Not surprising, the photo was of a well-endowed, topless woman in jeans and work boots seated on a forklift.

Ten Scavengers milled around the office, seven men and three women. An overweight man with a three-day growth of beard looked up from the desk as they entered.

"What do we have here?"

Tony shoved Monica into the center of the room. "We have a new team member for you."

"Good. I love fresh meat. Is she up to it?"

"If she gets bit, shoot her."

Monica wanted to spit on Tony but knew better. "I'm right here."

"Feisty little bitch," said the overweight man.

"That's why she's here. The Boss is hoping a few weeks in

The Pit might knock some of the fight out of her."

The overweight man stood and walked around the desk, standing in front of Monica. He was six inches taller than her.

"I'm Devon. I'm in charge of The Pit. Do what the others tell you and you'll be fine. Fuck up and you're dead. You get any of my team killed in the process, you'll pray you died in the accident. Clear?"

Monica said nothing.

Devon slapped her across the face. "Is that clear?"

"Yes." She practically growled her response.

"She's yours now." Tony leaned over to Monica and whispered, "Just do as they tell you and you'll be okay."

Once he and the escort left, Devon turned to the others. "Okay, gear up. We have a dozen new deaders to prep. Renee, you show the FNG the ropes."

"FNG?" asked Monica.

"Fucking New Guy." Renee stepped forward. About the same size as Monica, she had long, red hair tied in a ponytail and wore glasses, the right lens of which had a crack running down it. She had once been pretty but months of abuse had taken its toll. Dark circles under her eyes and the vacant stare indicated what she must have gone through. She seemed to have given up on life.

Devon unlocked the padlocks. Five men each took a semi-automatic rifle. Devon unlocked a file cabinet in the corner and removed five olive green bags containing ammunition. Those with weapons inserted magazines and exited through the interior door. The remaining three men and the other woman followed. Renee motioned for Monica to join them.

Devon sat back down behind his desk and laughed. "Have fun, bitch."

Monica glared at him. Renee took her arm and gently led her away, whispering in her ear, "Don't piss off Devon. He'll gladly make your time here an even greater Hell than it already is."

The five armed men had climbed a ladder up to a walkway that ran along the walls, positioning themselves at ten feet intervals. Monica barely noticed, her attention drawn to the ungodly groaning from two sets of cages erected by the sliding doors. Both cages were made from chain link fences, each ten feet tall with chain link roofs over them. Rebar had been welded horizontally to the posts every six inches to reinforce the structures, a necessity since the cages contained deaders. The larger of the cages, set on the opposite side of the garage, ran the length of the building from the farthest sliding door to the rear wall. It contained over a hundred deaders packed in tight. Off to their left sat the smaller of the two cages. It was half the size and stood in front of the first sliding door. Twelve deaders milled around inside. All of them rushed the cages, snarling and snapping their teeth at the food that remained out of reach.

The three men each held a four-foot-long animal catch pole. The woman clutched a cattle prod in her hands. All of them had donned leather jackets, leather gloves, and head gear used by riot police. Renee led Monica over to a folding table in the middle of the room. She handed Monica an identical set of gear. As Monica dressed, Renee opened the box. Twelve coils of something she did not recognize sat inside. Each was two feet long and had a device on the end with two lights, one red and one green. The red one glowed.

"What are these?" asked Monica.

"Primer chords. You'll be wrapping these around the deaders' necks."

"You can't be serious."

"Don't worry. We'll restrain them while you do it. It's easy." Renee dressed up in her gear and turned to the others. "Bring out the first one."

In front of each cage stood a smaller one, five feet square, made of the same chain link and rebar. A gate from the main cage led into the smaller one, with the exit into the garage opposite it. The Scavengers with the catch poles stood in a semi-circle around the outer gate. The woman stood by the side of the smaller cage, the tip of the cattle prod resting on one of the rebar supports. Renee unlocked and removed the outer padlock, lifted the fork latch, and stepped over to the main cage. The deaders lunged for her. Teeth bit against metal, decayed fingers reached through the fence.

"Terry, are you ready?"

The woman with the cattle prod nodded.

Renee unlocked and removed the inner padlock then quickly retreated out of the cage, closing the outer gate behind her. Using a pulley system, she raised the fork latch on the inner gate. A female deader in a blood-soaked Burger King uniform pushed its way into the smaller cage. A second deader in a Colorado State Patrol uniform attempted to push through. Terry shoved the cattle prod into its face. An electric shock ran through its head, disorienting the thing. Terry used the prod to push it back. When it was clear of the opening, Renee utilized the pulley system to close the inner gate and lower the fork latch. She stepped over to the outer gate and grabbed the latch.

"Eddie?"

The taller of the three men holding the catch poles said, "Let's get this over with."

Renee raised the latch and opened the gate a foot. The deader lunged at the gate, its right arm pushing through the opening. Renee leaned against the gate so the deader couldn't bust through. Eddie placed the pole around its wrist and tightened the loop.

"Secure."

"Roger that," said Renee. "Paul, you're up."

Paul maneuvered his pole through the opening and looped it around the deader's left arm.

"Secure."

"Roger that. Vince."

Vince stepped between the other two and tried to land the

loop on its forehead. It thrashed its head around, snapping at him with its teeth.

"Zap the motherfucker."

Terry placed the cattle prod against its chest and shocked it. The body stiffened long enough for enough Vince to close the loop around the deader's forehead. Renee opened the door, allowing the others to drag the creature out into the center of the garage. Terry stood close by with the prod.

Monica froze, her mind not grasping the insanity that played itself out in front of her.

Renee glanced over her shoulder at Monica. "What are you waiting for? Put on the collar."

Pulling one out of the box, she ran over to the deader. It lunged. She jumped back. It would have bitten her if the catcher poles hadn't held it in place.

"Do it from behind," suggested Renee.

Monica moved to the deader's rear, wrapped the chord around its neck twice, securing it in place with a strand of Velcro attached to the back of the detonator. When finished, she stepped back and raised her arms.

"Done."

Renee came over and examined the collar. She patted Monica on the shoulder. "Good job. Okay, people. Let's move this one over to the main cage."

The procedure for transferring the deader played out the same. Renee unlocked both doors to the smaller cage. The handlers placed the deader inside. Renee locked and secured the outer gate, then she used pulleys to open the inner one as Terry pushed it inside with the cattle prod. Once the transfer was complete and the gates to the main cage secured, the team went back to retrieve the next deader.

This time they chose a bloated male deader. Nobody would ever describe a deader as attractive, but this one made the rest look like prom queens. It had a size seventy waist, at least. The lower half was naked except for a pair of heavily soiled briefs that strained around its crotch and hips. Its bare feet were flattened by supporting the immense weight and left a small trail of blood wherever it sauntered. The deader wore a tattered white dress shirt five sizes too small. Only the button by the neck remained attached. The rest of the shirt, or what remained of it, had been pushed aside by the extended stomach and hung by its sides. Its face appeared as if it had been beaten with an ugly stick since day one of the outbreak. A piece of half-chewed flesh dangled from its mouth and down its chin.

"Christ," complained Vince. "Can't we dump this mother-fucker out back?"

Renee chuckled. "Do you want to go ask Devon that?"

"Fuck it. Let's get this over with."

Renee opened the inner gate and the bloated deader stumbled out. Terry kept the others at bay. When Renee opened the outer gate a foot, the guys looped its wrist and forehead, then led it outside into the garage. Monica came up from behind and began to wrap the primer chord around its neck.

Sensing fresh meat behind it, the deader spun around to get at her. Monica jumped back several feet to escape its snapping mouth. Because of its massive size, it pulled the poles strapped to its wrists from Vince's and Paul's hands. Only Eddie heled onto it by its forehead, and he would only be able to do so for a few seconds.

Terry rushed forward, placed the cattle prod against its stomach, and shocked it. The deader howled but did not stop thrashing around. It turned to Terry and lunged. She shoved the cattle prod harder and shocked it again.

The deader's bloated stomach burst open. Chunks of undigested flesh plopped out onto the floor, intermixing with decayed bodily fluids. The most foul-smelling stench Monica had ever experienced filled the garage. She ran over to the smaller cage, placed her hand on the bars, and vomited. Dozens of dead fingers pushed through the rebar and chain links, clutching for her hand. Monica backed away. She felt a stream of urine flow down her leg.

One of the guards on the catwalk yelled, "Clear the area!"

Everyone backed as far away from the deader as possible. Five streams of semi-automatic fire ripped into the thing, tearing it apart. The deader collapsed onto the floor. Eddie rushed over and stomped its head three times, making certain it would not get up.

The door to the office opened and Devin came out. "What the fuck is going… Christ, that stinks. Did the new bitch fuck up?"

"No," said Paul. "This one was too big to handle. It broke loose."

"Fuck." Devin thought for a moment. "Air this fucking place out. Have the FNG clean up the mess and then continue. And make it quick. I don't want to be here all night."

Devin returned to his office. Terry stepped over to the front of the garage and raised the center sliding door. The fresh air offered a welcome relief.

Renee glanced up at the walkway and waved. "Thanks."

The leader of the guards offered a half-hearted salute.

Vince moved over to the corpse and lifted it by the shoulders. "This fucking thing is heavy. New girl, help me."

Monica hesitated.

"Come on."

She came over and picked up its right leg. Vince picked up the left. The three of them half carried, half dragged the body outside and over to a pit fifty feet from the garage. As they tossed it in, Monica noticed the maggot-ridden corpses of several other deaders that had been put down in the same manner. When they tossed the body onto the pile, a swarm of massive black flies flew away, hovering around the three humans.

As they came back inside, Renee was moving a fifty-five-gallon drum over to the mound of human detritus while Terry used a broom to push the scattered pieces together. When

Monica approached, Terry handed her the broom and a shovel, and lowered her head.

"Sorry about this."

Monica swept the chunks of eaten, decayed flesh into the shovel, fighting back the urge to vomit again. Her throat hurt from the gagging, her pants were soaked, and the stench of death filled her nose.

Monica wished she had been killed during the ambush.

Chapter Nine

SLADE LAY IN bed staring at the ceiling. Despite a vigorous fuck, he still could not relax and fall to sleep. At first, he thought it might be the meds. He had taken a double dose of Viagra to ensure he was good to go, then spent the next thirty minutes pounding Gina's ass before the effects wore off. Maybe it was the frustration of not getting off. Or her laying beside him with her back to him, silently crying into her pillow until she fell asleep. Slade didn't know. Staying in bed and not being able to sleep did nothing but waste valuable time.

Swinging his legs out of bed, Slade got up and strolled over to the window overlooking the parking lot. Ahead of him sat The Pit and, though he could not see them from this angle, the factory and warehouse that housed his team and kept this all going. In the distance, moonlight reflected off the surface of the twin reservoirs. He had no clue how to refer to this. His domain? Territory? Turf? Operation? Not that it mattered. It belonged to him, including the seventeen hundred people who ran this set-up.

Not too shabby for a guy who was in prison when the outbreak occurred.

Back in the days before humanity fell apart, when he lived in Los Angeles, no one would have ever thought Slade would succeed at anything other than being a pain in the ass. Not his family, friends, that cunt wife of his, or the courts and local police. And in the time before the ends of days, he would not have. Slade never fit into "normal society," whatever the fucking hell that referred to. He got poor grades in school, but what it had mattered if he had gotten good ones? That lazy asshole who fathered him wouldn't have helped him get into college. Slade had what counted most in life – street smarts. He quickly learned that to survive you had to be tough and willing to dole out abuse, always quoting the line Sean Connery used in *The Untouchables* about if they send one of yours to the hospital you send one of theirs to the morgue. Sure, he could have done what most of his buddies did after high school and pick up some meaningless nine-to-five job where he got shit on all day by some college graduate in a suit only to go home with a small paycheck that had to support a wife and kids, but he was better than that. And smarter. So, he started dealing drugs.

Those five years were awesome. Within the first eighteen months, Slade had climbed his way to the top of drug syndicates in the city, mostly on the corpses of the other gangs he wiped out. With power came money, and with money came the good lifestyle and all the pussy he could handle. Then it all came crashing down when the city tried to clean up its streets and he found himself doing fifty to life in the state penitentiary. He had a lot of enemies within those walls and, thankfully, a few close associates who covered his back and several fellow inmates who helped him rather than have their families sliced up if they refused. Everything he had achieved kept him alive on the inside, though he missed the good life. Still, he was alive and that was all that mattered.

Eight years into his sentence, luck broke Slade's way when the dead came back to life and ravaged Los Angeles. The virus found its way into Lancaster Prison where he was being incarcerated. The inmates reanimated, turning on those within the cells. No way would Slade sit around and wait to become a happy meal for a flesh eater, or worse, find himself trapped inside a jail cell surrounded by the living dead. He organized a breakout, taking advantage of the chaos and using guards and weaker prisoners as bait, fighting his way to safety along with fifty other inmates, only nine of whom made it. Once free, he headed east into the desert. The only person he took with him was Mauler. He had to. Mauler was his little brother.

Though twice the size of Slade, Little Jimmy lacked the toughness or brains of his older brother. Their asshole of a father had no use for Little Jimmy and used to smack him around. When Slade landed in prison, the old man started wailing the shit out of Little Jimmy and molesting him to show his son – his own fucking son, for Christ's sake – who was boss. Abuse like that is going to fuck up anyone. Predictably, Little Jimmy became a bully in school and was eventually expelled in his sophomore year. The military rejected him because of his psych profile. The kid got in trouble, having a dozen assault charges filed against him within three years. When Little Jimmy repeatedly sodomized and dismembered a ten-year-old boy, the state finally locked him away in the looney bin. After Slade made his escape, he rescued Little Jimmy and brought him along so he could keep an eye on him. He started calling Little Jimmy by the name Mauler so no one would know they were related and because of the damage he could inflict when big brother told him to.

The two of them had moved east to escape the over-populated west coast only to find a power vacuum out here, a situation Slade quickly worked to remedy. He joined forces with others in the area looking to exploit the situation – biker gangs, drug cartels, but mostly scum like looters and thieves. He took them in because he needed the numbers and, under his leadership, they kept themselves under control. Anyone who tried to exert leadership over the group was taken down publicly, quickly, and violently.

What truly solidified his leadership was an incident that occurred two months ago when a rival MS-13 gang from Denver moved into Slade's turf. Slade sent out a delegation of five to negotiate a deal with their leader. Their leader sent back the heads of the five delegates in a plastic garbage bag. Three nights later, Slade and his group paid MS-13 a visit, beheaded each of the gang members, and stuck their heads on pikes outside the MS-13 compound. Everyone else in the area got the message.

Yet Slade knew that rule by fear would not keep him in power for long. He brought into the group people who would normally be terrified of him – families, young couples, professionals. He gave them a safe place to sleep, food, and protection. They did the work the roughnecks couldn't, using their skill sets to keep the compound going. Once, when three of the bikers raped a sixteen-year-old, Slade allowed her father and older brother to beat the assholes to death with baseball bats in front of the others. It had the desired effect. The roughnecks learned their place. Big Jake established the brothel where the roughnecks could do whatever they wanted as long as they didn't hurt anyone in the group. The others felt safe, both from deaders and the less desirable elements among them, and worked extra hard to keep it that way.

Things had been going well these past two months. Yet one thing still boded ill for the future – the new government set up in White Sands, New Mexico, five hundred miles south of them. Once the new administration had built up enough troops and supplies, they would attempt to take back the United States. Slade was as patriotic as anyone else, but their drive to clear away deaders would encroach on the domain he had struggled so hard to set up. He couldn't allow that. It was why he had started raiding their territory, ambushing rail shipments, derailing trains, and preventing much needed material and personnel from reaching New Mexico. Soon he would send raiding parties farther south to cut off road access between St. Louis and White Sands, which would place a strain on his people and their resources. But it had to be done. Slade had to keep them off balance at least for a few more months until he was able to launch his own plan to ensure dominance. If successful, it would be Slade running the post-apocalypse United States, not the government in White Sands.

Chapter Ten

ALISSA, NATHAN, AND Chris joined Whitaker for the morning briefing on their trip to Albuquerque. Two others joined them, a middle-aged man in grease-stained overalls and a young blonde woman in desert-colored military fatigues with no rank.

"I'll make this quick," said Whitaker. He pointed to the man. "This is Rogers. He's your engineer for this trip."

He tipped his hat to the newcomers. "Howdy."

"The young lady is Charlotte. She's heading up the security detail who'll accompany you."

Charlotte nodded.

"You'll be going to the usual pick-up point at the junction with Route 15 north of Newton."

"Where's that?" asked Chris.

"A little over twenty miles north of Wichita, Kansas."

"Can't you get us any closer to White Sands?" asked Alissa.

"Not anymore. We used to run a train on a branch line that by-passed the major cities and took us into Colorado, then picked up a major line that took us to Albuquerque. The Scavengers ambushed a train yesterday in Hutchinson, derailing it and stealing the supplies on board. That route is now unusable."

"I assume going through major cities is out," said Chris.

"Oh, yeah." Rogers chuckled.

"Are the deaders that bad?"

"I can push through deaders with no problem. There are

too many obstructions on the tracks. We run too great a risk of getting stuck."

Whitaker continued. "The route you're taking is the safest out of the area. Rogers, we have reports of heavy deader activity on the tracks between us and Kansas City, so I'm putting Gretchen in the lead."

"Sounds good to me.'

"Who's Gretchen?" asked Alissa.

"Not who, but what. Gretchen the Grinder. It's a rotary track snowplow. Works great on the living dead."

"Will I have drone support?" asked Rogers.

"Unfortunately, no. We lost it when the Scavengers derailed the train. Abney's people checked the area around the pick-up point and report it clear." Whitaker focused his attention on Alissa. "Abney is the leader of the group who'll escort you to White Sands."

"Are they trustworthy?" asked Alissa.

"They're the best team of rovers we have out there."

Charlotte snorted. "They're weird."

"How so?"

"You'll find out when you meet them. They're unique but excellent at their job." Rogers glanced around the room. "Are there any questions?"

No one spoke.

"Good. Miss Madison, your people are already aboard the train. Rogers and Charlotte will show you the way. Best of luck to all of you. For everyone's sake, I hope those blood samples can produce a vaccine."

THEIR TRAIN SAT on a siding by the perimeter wall. It consisted of one Amtrak rail car occupied by her people and the other nineteen members of the security team, a diesel engine, and Gretchen, an antique steam-powered rotary snowplow.

Nathan, Chris, and Charlotte climbed aboard the rail car and Rogers made his way to the engine.

Woody and Ben waited for her.

"Are you two joining us?" she asked.

"No," said Woody. "Ben and I decided to stay here where we can be of better use. We wanted to say goodbye and wish you luck."

"Thank you." Alissa hugged Woody, which caught him off guard.

"You're welcome."

Alissa stepped over and hugged Ben. "And thank you for putting your lives on the line for us on Warren Island. None of us would be here without the two of you."

"Our pleasure." Ben embraced her.

Alissa watched the two men walk away. Curiosity got the better of her and she went over to examine Gretchen.

It was constructed of wood painted dark red. The words ROTARY O Y were painted in white on the side. Black smoke rose from one of the open hatches on its roof. What made the car stand out was the device mounted up front. A cylindrical metal structure the width of the tracks, with a square metal catcher, the sides of which extended two feet beyond the track. She stepped around front. Inside the cylinder sat a circular rotor with spikes designed to catch snow and blades to break it up. She could only imagine the effect this would have on any deaders blocking their path.

An older gentleman, thin with snow white hair, came around the other side of Gretchen. He wore regular civilian clothes and wiped his hands on a soiled handkerchief.

"Pretty impressive, huh?"

"I'll say," answered Alissa. "Have you used it before?"

"Quite a few times. Ole Gretchen here is a seasoned veteran of the deader war." He shoved the handkerchief into his pants pocket then offered his hand. "I'm Steam. I take care of the old girl."

She shook his hand. "Alissa."

"You're the head of the group we're taking to meet Abney."

"I am."

"You're welcome to ride with me if you want."

"Are you sure?"

"I can use the company. It gets lonely up here. This way I can show you what she's capable of."

Steam ushered her aboard. She was surprised at how spartan the inside appeared. The boiler took up two-thirds of the car, making the interior at least twenty degrees warmer. The only other items were a series of gears and levers on the front wall to control the rotary plow and a block of wood with a cushion on top nailed to the floor to provide a seat for Steam. She slid off her leather jacket and placed it on a hook mounted on the wall. Steam picked up a two-way radio.

"Ready when you are. The young lady is riding with me."

"Roger that. Let's roll."

The diesel engine gave two blasts from its air horn. A tractor trailer blocking the entrance started up. Steel sheets reinforced with rebar had been welded to the right side of the truck to prevent anything from getting in. The truck rolled forward, clearing a gap in the container defenses. The train lurched and began to inch forward, slowly leaving the compound. Once they had departed, the truck moved back in position, closing the defenses.

Steam made himself as comfortable as possible. He pointed to a folding down chair on the wall to his left.

"Relax and enjoy the ride. It'll be a while before we run into any deaders."

AN HOUR ELAPSED without incident. The farther they got from St. Louis, the more the scenery became of an endless landscape of farms, broken occasionally by houses or barns. Between that and the gentle swaying of the train, Alissa's thoughts soon drifted away from her usual planning and overthinking every single move to a more casual flow. She began to compare their former situation at the cabin with here. While well stocked, as recent events had shown the cabin was far from secure and other options were limited. Out here the country was open and the population much less than the coast, so the opportunities for survival seemed greater. From what everyone said, White Sands seemed the ideal location to rebuild society and hopefully take back the country from the living dead. Sure, the chances of an outbreak occurring and spreading were greater in a more densely populated environment, but in this case the advantages outweighed the risks. Alissa began to feel more comfortable with her decision to move the group out here.

Alissa also began to realize how lucky they had been, the nightmares in Boston, Nahant, and Warren Island notwithstanding. Seeing that massive swarm of deaders massing along the Mississippi River brought home to her how terrible the situation throughout the country had been. She was lucky to have been living in a less populated area. She pitied the people of Chicago, New York City, and the Washington area as well as anyone caught along the mid-Atlantic seacoast. She could imagine the nightmare the survivors had gone through, assuming anyone had survived.

Her biggest issue now, and one she tried to avoid, was how to handle her relationship with Nathan and Chris. Sure, she had dated two guys at once, but never guys who knew each other, let alone been within her closest circle of friends, and never during an apocalyptic situation where the odds of living were stacked against them. Alissa cared for them both. Yet a love triangle in such this situation could erode the cohesion of her group, which had become her primary concern. It was the first time in her life she felt needed. Which only figures, because it was also the first time in her life she had to weigh her own desires against the good of the group. Sadly, she might have to put her—

"It's showtime," said Steam.

"What?"

He pointed ahead of them.

Alissa leaned out of the cab and glanced down the tracks. Close to one hundred deaders shambled toward them, most between the twin rails, their hands reaching out to feed, unaware of what would soon happen.

Steam stepped over to the gears. As he manipulated levers with his left hand, with his right he picked up the two-way radio and warned the others. "Hang on. Things are about to get messy."

Pressure from the boilers flowed through the pipes and into the gear box. The outside rotor began spinning. The sound of metal scratching against metal filled the cabin, replaced seconds later by a clanking whir as the plow spun into full rotation. Alissa focused her attention on the deaders now only a hundred feet away.

The train lurched slightly as it impacted against the horde. Limbs spun out of the side of the rim, somersaulting before landing on the side of the tracks and bouncing several times before rolling to a stop. A rattling inside the rotor housing made its way up the chute located at the top of the plow and pointed left. Moments later, sliced body parts and congealed blood vomited from the top of the chute, spraying the ground in a sickening rain of gore. Alissa stepped back to avoid being splashed. Even inside the cab, she could smell the stench of decay and rotten bodily fluids and heard the groaning of deaders as they went through the meatgrinder. The slaughter ended in a matter of seconds. Alissa peered out the side window, looking to the rear. A bloody trail over two hundred feet long lay behind them. Damn, these people know what they were doing.

Steam picked up the radio again. "All clear. Next stop is the rendezvous with Abney."

Chapter Eleven

T HE NEXT FOUR hours passed by without incident, which suited Alissa fine. The stench of the pack of deaders they had sliced and diced still permeated the cab. As she leaned out the window, watching the farmland drift by, she spotted several vehicles parked at the next railroad crossing.

"I think we have trouble ahead."

Steam came over and checked. "Nope. That's Abney's people, right on time, as always."

The train slowed, eventually coming to a stop with the diesel engine stretched across Route 15. Rogers climbed down from his cab, stooped under the crossing arm, and greeted one of them with a manly hug. Alissa climbed down from her cab and moved to the back to join her group. Charlotte's security team had already deployed in a circle around the perimeter, prepared for trouble, though it did not appear as if they would run into any. Nathan and Chris disembarked next.

Chris stared at those parked on the road, his mouth slightly agape. "You gotta be fucking kidding."

Alissa agreed. She had been expecting a para-military group, retired police, or preppers. These people fit none of those descriptions. She understood now what Charlotte meant when she called them weird. They looked like they had just come from a comic book convention. They wore clothes that were a combination of steampunk and low-budget post-apocalypse movies. From this distance they all seemed young, in their mid-twenties to mid-thirties. Despite their youth and the outlandish costumes, she sensed a good vibe coming from them. Not cockiness but confidence. Each carried a sidearm. She assumed the heavy weapons were in the vehicles.

The vehicles were a sight to behold. The lead car was a four-door, midnight black Dodge Ram that had seen better days. Four metal rods had been welded to the front, extending over the hood, windshield, and roof and ending on the end of the bed. Sharpened strips of steel, essentially three-foot-long blades, had been welded at an angle along the side of the tops of the bed and rear chassis. Steel plates had been welded to the fenders, doors, and hood, the former covering the tires. Skull and crossbones had been painted in white on the hood. Behind it sat a 1970s-era VW minibus. Rebar covered the exterior of the windows and steel plates all four sides. An ambulance sat third in line, looking normal except for a loudspeaker mounted on the roof. Music played softly. It sounded like something that would be heard in a Middle Eastern bizarre. Off to the left stood a World War II-era military jeep with twin .50 caliber machine guns attached to a tripod covered by a plate of steel with view slits for the gunner. Four steel plates formed a pit around the tripod. Two Harley Davidson motorcycles sat on either side of the convoy, all four of them weathered from constant use. The only vehicle that appeared semi-normal was a yellow school bus that had wire mesh welded over the side windows and steel plates welded to the exterior.

Kiera stepped off the train, her eyes widening when she saw their means of transportation. "Fucking awesome."

"Language, young lady," chastised Miriam.

Steam escorted the leader of the group over to them. He was of average height and build and, although not Hollywood attractive, could still be considered good looking, an appearance enhanced by his smile. He wore jeans, a denim light blue shirt, and work boots covered by a worn, thin leather overcoat. Alissa noticed he carried a sawed-off double barrel shotgun in a holster around his waist. His dark hair hung down to his shoulders covering a red handkerchief around his neck.

A stunningly beautiful redhead broke away from the convoy and joined them. She wore knee high leather boots and a leather biker's jacket that stopped at her waist. Her hair flowed halfway down her back.

"I'm going to enjoy this trip," Chris whispered to Nathan.

Steam made the introductions. "This is Alissa, the leader of the group you'll be taking to White Sands. This is Abney. He's in charge of your escort."

Abney offered his hand. "It's a pleasure to meet you."

Alissa shook it. "Same here."

"Don't let their appearance fool you," said Steam. "They're the best desert runners around. I can vouch for them personally. They got my wife, daughter, and grandson safely to White Sands despite all the dangers."

"You come highly recommended." Alissa did not know what else to say.

The redhead extended her hand. "I'm Lindsey."

"Nice to meet you."

Shithead bounded off the train and raced over to his master. Upon seeing Abney and Lindsey, he broke off to say hello. Abney bent over and scratched the dog's behind. The tail wagged furiously. "What's his name?"

"Shithead?" Chris answered.

Abney laughed. "I'm sure it's a name welled earned."

The children disembarked next. Lindsey's eyes lit up. She went over and crouched before them. "Hello. I'm Lindsey. What's your names?"

"Little Stevie."

"Connie."

"Susie." Embarrassed, she averted her gaze.

"I bet you three have had a lot of adventures since this all began."

The kids nodded. Little Stevie said, "You wouldn't believe how many deaders we've killed."

"Really?" Lindsey smiled. "You'll have to tell me tonight over dinner."

As Lindsey chatted with the kids, Abney asked, "Where's your gear?"

"Aboard the train." Alissa turned to Nathan and Chris. "We'll get it."

"We'll take care of it." Abney called out to the convoy. "Tupoc?"

A large man answered in a burly voice. "What's up?"

"Grab their gear and store it on the bus."

"Gotcha."

Tupoc and seven others came over to the train.

"Be careful of Archer," said Alissa.

"Who's Archer?"

"My cat. He's in a carrier. He can be a bit ornery."

"Gotcha."

Lindsey stood. "If you follow me, I'll get you settled on the bus."

"Thank you." Miriam ushered along the kids. The others fell in behind her.

"I can take two of you in the pick-up with me," said Abney.

"You go," Chris offered Nathan. "I'll ride in the bus with Shithead."

The dog responded with a bark and a wagging tail.

Nathan smiled. "I guess I'm riding shotgun."

"Sorry, but that honor is reserved for Lindsey. You two will have to ride in back. Just enjoy the scenery." Abney stepped over and hugged Steam again. "I'll tell your family you said hello."

"Thanks. And tell them I love them." Steam focused his attention on Alissa. "Good luck. You're in good hands. Trust me."

"Thanks for everything."

"Are we almost ready?" Rogers asked from the cab of the diesel engine. "I want to be back at Oregon Trail Prime by dusk."

"We are," answered Steam. He returned to Gretchen.

Rogers reached in and blew the whistle once. Charlotte's team fell back and boarded the Amtrak railcar. When the last guard was aboard, Charlotte waved to Rogers, who waved back, then jumped aboard the train. A few seconds later, the train lurched into reverse and backed down the tracks the way they had come. Alissa watched until it became a small dot in the distance.

Abney approached Alissa from behind. "We're ready when you are."

"Coming." She followed Abney to the Ram and climbed in back beside Nathan.

Abney started the pick-up and swung it into a U-turn. The rest of the convoy followed. They headed south.

Chapter Twelve

DESPITE DRIVING FOR over an hour, the landscape never seemed to changed. Considering the convoy drove through farm country untended for four months, each mile looked like those they had already passed and the ones they would drive by for God knows how long. Alissa had worked with two interns from the Midwest. One always said that the scenery down here was the most monotonous anywhere in the country, and that you could drive for hundreds of miles and see nothing but farmland. The other intern would correct her, arguing the view wasn't monotonous. Sometimes you saw cornfields, other times wheat. Only now did Alissa realize they weren't joking.

At one point, Alissa noticed Abney and Lindsey were holding hands. Every so often, she would glance over at him and smile, a look of pure admiration in her eyes. Alissa remembered when Paul used to look at her that way during the first few years of their relationship before things soured between them. A part of her envied those days.

The convoy passed through a small town. She didn't catch its name. The main thoroughfare stretched for less than half a mile, with side roads that ended after one block. Commercial buildings lined the main road, with houses behind them. Neither the living nor living dead could be seen. The outbreak had reached this far. A few abandoned vehicles blocked the road while others sat in parking spaces, their doors open. Garbage and discarded items, occasionally luggage, littered the streets. Every store that contained essential supplies had been ransacked – the grocery store, hardware store, pharmacy, liquor store, gun shop, and doctor's office. Each door had a large X painted in red across it. Three piles of corpses sat in front of city hall, each pile having been burned, leaving nothing but charred corpses. Alissa wondered what nightmare the residents had endured.

Once past town, Lindsey opened a map and studied it. "You'll want to take the road several miles down on the left."

"Does it give a name?" he asked.

"No, but it's the only road for miles."

A few minutes later, Abney said, "Oh, yeah, I remember this place. We got the first house but didn't get a chance to check out the second."

Lindsey reached out and rubbed his leg.

At the intersection, Abney turned left. After a few miles, the convoy passed a ranch-style house off to the right. The front door had been left ajar and a large X painted across it in red, like in town. Alissa pointed it out.

"Is that where we're going?"

Lindsey shifted in his seat so she could chat with Alissa. "No. We got that house last month. There's another one at the end of the road we didn't see last time."

"Do you do this for the military?" asked Nathan.

"This is on our own time. Don't worry, though. It won't take long. We'll still get you to White Sands tomorrow."

Lindsey spun around to face front. Nathan faced Alissa, his expression implying he was worried about this side venture. Alissa felt more curiosity than trepidation.

Half an hour later a farm appeared on the horizon, a two-story house with a hundred acres of farmland behind it. Someone had sown the crops since the outbreak. Off to the left stood a red-painted stable with a fenced in area surrounding it. The gate remained closed. A silo stood off to the right. Alissa studied the property for signs of life but saw none.

The convoy stopped in front of the house. Abney and Lindsey climbed out. Alissa and Nathan joined them. A woman exited the ambulance to join them. She was an attractive woman with blonde hair and a little older than Abney. She wore sand-colored military-style pants and an olive drab t-shirt, a French Foreign Legion hat with a back covering that shielded her neck and hair, and a tan handkerchief tied around her neck. She carried an axe as a weapon. As they approached the house, Alissa noticed that the front and screen doors had been left open. A snarl came from inside. Everyone stopped. Alissa and Nathan pulled the Carbines off their shoulder. None of the others seemed concerned.

A deader centered itself in the doorway, a young man, probably in his mid-twenties. He wore nice clothes, his polyester shirt stained down the left arm and back with blood. While human, he had tried to commit suicide by shooting himself in the head. Either his aim had been off or the weapon had been of a small caliber, and he only succeeded in blasting off the top left side of his skull. The bullet had missed the primordial nervous system that drove the deaders. Judging by the lack of decay, this was one of the recent dead, which meant they faced a runner. Alissa raised her weapon to fire.

Lindsey stopped her. "We got this."

"Joan?" asked Abney.

"I'm on it." Joan stepped forward a few paces, raised the axe above her head, and whistled.

The deader focused on her, snarled, and charged. Joan judged the distance and threw the axe. It somersaulted once before the blade struck the deader in the center of its forehead, slicing half-way through its skull. It continued charging for a few more feet before it collapsed in front of Joan. She stepped forward, placed her foot on its chest, and yanked the axe free.

"I don't believe it," mumbled Nathan.

"You should." Abney grinned like a kid on Christmas morning. "That's Joan MacLeod, axe throwing champion for

Clay County for three years in a row."

Joan gave him a thumbs up before wiping the blade off on the deader's shirt.

Movement came from inside the house, followed by sound. Not the snarl of a deader but a scared yip. A moment later, the tiny tan head of a nine-month-old Labrador Retriever stuck its head around the jamb, carefully eyeing the newcomers.

"Oh, he's adorable." Lindsey dropped to her knees and patted her leg with her right hand. "Come here, boy."

The dog hesitated, its eyes fixed on the deader.

"Come on, boy. It's okay."

The puppy inched his way onto the porch, stared one more time at the deader, then raced over to Lindsey, its tail wagging furiously. Lindsey held out her arms. The Lab jumped on her and cuddled for protection. She hugged it close and petted its head. The dog responded with a face bath.

"You're a good boy. What's your name?" She tried to read his collar, finally finding the tag. It read Thor. "Thor? What a tough name for someone so cute."

Nathan chuckled.

"What's so funny?" asked Alissa.

"It's a LabraThor."

Abney laughed out loud.

"Don't listen to the bad man," said Lindsey in a baby voice. "That's a beautiful name."

Abney came over to pet the dog. "You made another friend."

"They deserve to be saved, too."

He turned to the others. "Tupoc, set up a perimeter about a mile out. Let me know if you spot any danger."

Tupoc saluted and the four motorcycles headed out, one in each compass direction.

"Shall we see what's inside?" asked Abney.

The other nodded and followed him into the house.

The stench of death permeated the interior. Two bodies sat

in the side-by-side recliners in the living room. Neither moved. Two pools of blood stained the carpet on either side of the bodies. Alissa walked over and examined them. Judging by the few tuffs of white hair on their scalps and the canes by the chairs, these two were much older than the deader that had attacked them. They held hands. Their faces had been eaten away, but that had not been the cause of death. Two long, deep gashes ran down their right and left arms, respectively, from their upper forearms to their palms. An empty bottle of burgundy and two dirty wine classes sat on the dining room table. The couple had gotten drunk and taken their own lives.

Most of Abney's people and Alissa's group entered. Joan removed two blankets from the sofa and covered the couple. Abney focused on his team. "Malcolm?"

"Yeah?" Malcolm was a tall, lanky kid with blonde, naturally curly hair and acne on his cheeks and chin. Alissa guessed he was still in high school when the outbreak hit. He wore a waist-length flyer's leather jacket and a top hat with steampunk-style goggles wrapped above the brim.

"Gather up a party and dig three graves out back."

Malcolm nodded. "Anyone want to help?"

Nathan, Chris, and Steve volunteered. As they left, the children entered with Miriam. Upon seeing the puppy, they squealed and ran over to Lindsey.

"Can we play with him?" asked Connie.

"Sure." Lindsey handed Thor to them. "Be careful. He's scared."

Connie took the puppy, being rewarded with a face bath. The other kids joined in.

Shithead wandered in and crossed over to the children. He edged closer, stretched out his nose, and sniffed Thor. The puppy yipped. Shithead jumped back, but quickly moved forward and sniffed again. His tail wagged and he slopped his huge tongue on the puppy's head. Thor barked once and wagged his tail.

Carrington came in holding the cooler. "I'm going to check the freezer to see if they have ice I can add."

"Go ahead," said Abney.

As the others went about their business, Alissa went over the mantlepiece above the fireplace. Eight picture frames sat on it. Seven contained images of an older man and woman, presumably the couple that had committed suicide. One was a wedding photo from the 1970s. The others showed them posing in front of the farm, holding a baby swaddled in a blue blanket, and the rest taking the obligatory photoshoots in front of the Las Vegas sign and other landmarks she didn't recognize. The eighth photo caught her attention – the couple standing on either side of a young man in his late twenties who looked like the deader they had killed out front.

Curiosity getting the better of her, Alissa went over to the bodies laying in the recliner, removed the blankets, and checked for bite wounds. There were none other than the chewing of their faces. They must have given up and ended their lives on their own terms. She replaced the blankets and stepped outside to check the deader. It had no bite wounds either, although the right pants leg had been ripped open on the side and a gouge had been taken out of its leg. The gash had been caused by something but not sharp, like a bladed weapon. The area around the wound showed signs of the deader infection. She wondered how he had gotten it.

As Alissa headed back inside, she spotted Lindsey using a can of spray paint to place a large red X on the door.

"You're the ones putting an X on the doors."

"That's us."

"Why?"

"We check every building we come across for survivors and bury the dead, if we find any. If there's canned food and water, we leave it and note the location on a map. Hopefully, some of the stragglers out here will come across it and have a chance of survival."

"You're not Scavengers, are you?"

Lindsey snorted. "God forbid. Those assholes take every-thing they find for themselves and murder those who refuse to join them. We only take medicines and weapons for the folks at White Sands and a few luxuries for ourselves that we trade on the road for gas. We've also saved twenty to thirty pets left behind by their owners."

"What do you do with them?"

"We take them with us to White Sands. The people there love them. It brings a sense of normality to their lives." Lindsey met Alissa's gaze, her expression filled with compassion. "The world has become a horrible place since the dead came back to life. We're just trying to help out those who need it and bring a little decency back into the world."

One of Lindsey's team came back from checking the grain elevator. "Good news. The elevator is full of grain. As far as I can tell, it hasn't been ruined."

"Excellent. We'll tell them at White Sands. They can send out a truck to retrieve it. That'll feed a lot of people on base. Let's hope the Scavengers don't find it first."

Alissa went back inside. A cardboard box had been placed on the dining room table. In it were seven bottles of alcohol – Jim Beam, Captain Morgan, Absolut, and four unopened bottles of wine – plus half a box of cigars and all the prescrip-tion and over-the-counter medications that were found in the house. Nothing of a personal nature had been taken.

TWO HOURS LATER, the three bodies had been wrapped in blankets, placed in the graves dug out back, and covered over. Everyone had gathered in a semi-circle around their final resting place. Abney stepped over to the mounds.

"Heavenly Father, please take the souls of these victims of this nightmare and embrace them with Your love and care. We know that taking your own life is against the Scripture but, under the circumstances, we pray you'll forgive them and grant them salvation. Please bless those of us out here who are trying to do well by his fellow man. Bless us with Your grace and keep us safe. In Your name we pray. Amen."

Everyone in the group responded "Amen."

Lindsey stepped forward, crouched in front of the center grave, and placed something at the head of the mound. As she rejoined Abney, Alissa saw it was the photograph of the three deceased she had taken from the mantlepiece.

Abney turned to the two teams, his tone more commanding. "We're going to bunk down here for the night."

"We can't," protested Carrington. "We need to get these samples to White Sands as soon as possible."

"We'll never make it to New Mexico by sunset and it's too dangerous to drive at night." Abney interrupted the doctor when he tried to argue his case. "Trust me, it's better this way. We'll be at White Sands tomorrow."

Carrington gave in, knowing he would not win this argument.

"My people will stand watch tonight. We'll hit the road at dawn tomorrow."

"What about dinner?" asked Chris.

"We have enough food on the bus for dinner and breakfast. We'll take care of everything. By this time tomorrow you'll be in New Mexico."

Chapter Thirteen

D INNER THAT NIGHT consisted of canned food or MREs, with a limited variety of meats and pastas available, all of it provided by the military. No essential supplies were taken from the house except for logs to build an outdoor fire. After they ate, everyone chatted. Well, everyone but the kids. They took turns holding and doting on Thor, of course under the watchful eye of the puppy's adopted father, Shithead. Alissa had set up Archer in one of the spare bedrooms upstairs. The rest of them sat around talking, mostly about how they wound up here. No one discussed vaccines, cures, or Scavengers. It was all personal talk. And bad jokes. It turned out Abney had a dark sense of humor, like Chris, and way too many jokes and puns were exchanged. Not that anyone cared. For the first time since the smart deaders' attack on the cabin, Alissa felt like part of a family.

Abney and Lindsey both had lived in Santa Fe where she worked at a local animal shelter and he served as one of the city's animal control officers, which was how they met. When the deader outbreak took place, they made their way to the safety of the desert, eventually finding refuge at White Sands when the Speaker of the House set up the new government there. Neither of them felt comfortable due to the power struggle between the civilians and military, the organizational disarray, and the increasing number of displaced making their way into camp and bringing with them a greater chance of a second outbreak. After a few weeks, Abney and Lindsey had gathered a like-minded team and set off into the desert to fend for themselves. They scrounged around for means of transportation, suped them up for the apocalypse, and survived on the road. Fortunately, the group had enough eclectic experience that they beat the odds and thrived.

Tupoc, the head of the security detail, had been a security guard based out of Encino. He had been doing a double overnight shift in a warehouse thirty miles from the nearest town and, as such, had no clue society had fallen apart until his replacement never showed up to relieve him and his supervisor didn't answer his cell phone. At the end of his third shift, he abandoned his post and fended for himself until he joined up with Abney. Tupoc's team comprised Reg, a bouncer at a strip club outside of Vegas, close to three hundred pounds of muscle and a heart of gold, and Casey, one of the more attractive and popular entertainers. They were the only two to make it out and spent the next three weeks roaming the desert and avoiding deaders. Liam rounded out the team. They came across him near the Zuni Reservation, dehydrated and half dead, and Abney let him join the group. He never talked about his past and kept to himself. Liam was a ferocious fighter, showing no mercy to deaders but complete loyalty to his colleagues.

Kennedy drove the school bus. A single mother of three, she had driven one in her hometown of Tucson. On the day of the outbreak, she tried to save her children but failed, their schools having been overrun. Instead, she rescued as many other children as possible, packing them in her bus and driving them to the safety of White Sands before the new government established itself there. When Abney arrived with other survivors, Kennedy asked to go along. Brian, who drove the VW minibus that carried their supplies, had a similar story. He was a truck driver based out of Albuquerque who was in Wyoming when the shit hit the fan. Brian tried to get back to his wife and kids but couldn't make it through the gridlocked roads. He made it south of Cheyenne before Albuquerque fell to the living dead. Two weeks later he heard about Abney's team, tracked them down, and demanded they let him join so he could offer some payback to the things that had butchered his family.

Pops and Fifty-fifty oversaw the Jeep. Pops got his nickname being the oldest member of the team at forty-five. He had put in his twenty years in the Navy, retired, and lived outside of Lubbock, Texas with no wife, girlfriends, kids, or pets. When the dead came to life, Pops wanted a way to get back in the fight. Abney offered the best opportunity. Fifty-fifty, in his early twenties, had finished a two-year tour in the Navy and left his wife in San Diego to visit his folks in Chicago. When the outbreak hit, he tried to get home, making it as far as Denver before his car broke down. Chicago and San Diego fell to the deaders within days, taking both his families along with everyone else. Joining with Abney gave Fifty-fifty a chance to get some revenge.

Joan MacLeod, the axe throwing champion for Clay County, had been widowed by a drunk driver five years ago and never remarried. When things went south, she knew enough to get away from populated centers and headed west, holding up in an abandoned roadside diner until Abney found her.

The last member of the group tuned out to be the most fascinating. Malcolm was a senior in high school when the world went to hell. A self-described geek, he used to play video games, engaged in steampunk LARPing, and held anime watch parties with his friends on Saturday nights. His engineering abilities made him invaluable to the team. Malcolm had devised the protective defenses welded to the vehicles, put together the twin fifties mounted on the back of the Jeep, rigged up the stereo system on the ambulance, as well as lot more. He and three friends had taken a trip to Roswell the day the outbreak occurred. One committed suicide, two headed for Wyoming, and Malcolm tried to make it home. He failed.

Thankfully for everyone concerned, he eventually met up with Abney and his team.

Around nine o'clock, Abney called it a night and told everyone to rest up for tomorrow. Tupoc and his team drove off on their motorcycles to set up a security perimeter. Alissa, Nathan, Chris, and Steve volunteered to replace them in five hours. Kiera had wanted to go, but Alissa told her after everything she had been through, she needed to rest. Alissa had meant what she had said earlier about keeping the teenager out of harm's way as much as possible. Lindsey excused herself, saying she wanted to check on the stable.

Alissa went upstairs to check on Archer. She cuddled with him for a few minutes, enjoying his purring and his rubbing his head against her face. He then jumped out of her arms, went over to the bag near his carrier, plopped his ass down on the carpet, and meowed loudly until Alissa finally gave him food and water. No longer needed, she opted to take a tour of the farm and clear her head.

As Alissa passed by the stable, she heard crying coming from inside. Unslinging the Carbine from her shoulder, she held it in the high-ready position and entered.

Lindsey stood by the center stall, petting a horse, her head resting against its cheek as she petted him.

Alissa lowered the weapon. "Is everything okay?"

Lindsey raised her head. Her eyes were red from crying and tears streamed down her face. "I'm just upset."

"What's wrong?"

Lindsey pointed to the other two stalls. Each contained emaciated, dead horses. Flies and maggots had begun to consume the carcasses.

"The old couple had three horses and either forgot to feed them or were too scared to venture out on their own." Lindsey sniffed back her tears and wiped her eyes. "He's the only one to survive, barely. I gave him a bucket of water and some hay and he wolved them both down in minutes."

Alissa slung her Carbine back over her shoulder and joined Lindsey. The horse eyed her warily until she also petted him, then nudged her gently with his nose.

"I'm sorry."

"Thanks. I know it's foolish, but I hate to see animals suffer. Humans can fend for themselves, but not pets. You have no idea how many houses we've checked where we find the bodies of dead...."

Lindsey broke down again and excused herself. She gathered more hay and water. When she returned, she had regained her composure.

Lindsey hung the bucket of water on a hook inside the stable. The horse slurped it. "I don't mean to be so emotional."

"Don't be. Being emotional is what separates us from them."

"Do you mean the deaders or the Scavengers?"

"Both." Alissa could not help but recall their encounter with Dickson's group.

"That means a lot coming from you."

"What do you mean?"

Lindsey smiled. "I talked with the kids earlier. They told me how you rescued them from deaders or that gang that had kidnapped them in New Hampshire. How you drove to Maine to save your friend's life and flew into Boston to retrieve the blood for the vaccine. You're a hero to Susie for getting her off that island."

"I'm far from a hero."

"Now you're selling yourself short," chastised Lindsey. "Most of the people we run across are either too scared to function or are in it for themselves. You're the first group we've run into that's not selfish about what they do?"

"What do you mean selfish?"

"There's another group like ours, but when they check on homes they're looking for luxury items." Lindsey's expression became harsh. "There are a lot of elites at White Sands who pay big bucks for things like expensive clothes and jewelry, drugs, and porn. There's a huge black market for that stuff. Abney refuses to have any part of it. Too many people are struggling to survive for the wealthy to live their old lifestyle."

"You love him, don't you?"

Lindsey beamed. "We were engaged and planning our wedding when this shit broke out. It doesn't matter as long as we're together."

"I hear you."

"I only have one guy to keep in line. You have two."

Alissa rolled her eyes. "Is it that obvious?"

"It is to me, but I'm a woman. We're a lot smarter than the men we date." Lindsey offered a smile and a conspiratorial wink.

"I care for them both, but I don't want a love triangle getting in the way."

"I understand, but you also have to think of your own needs. None of us know how long we have." Lindsey changed topics. "Can I ask about your eye?"

Alissa involuntarily reached for the eyepatch. "A deader knocked me over on Warren Island and I hit my head. It knocked the retina loose. I have a huge black spot in my eye that screws up my vision. I'm hoping the doctors at White Sands can operate on it."

"It makes you look tough. And the guys like it."

"Bullshit."

"No, really." Lindsey leaned closer to share a secret. "Abney asked me if I'd be willing to wear one."

Both women laughed at the inside joke. After a few more minutes of chatting, they headed back to the farmhouse.

Chapter Fourteen

S LADE SAT IN the cafeteria talking with Mauler, Tony, and a few of the raiders when Gina rushed over and slid onto the bench beside him.

"I just got word from our source inside Oregon Trail Prime. They sent out a second convoy this morning to White Sands."

"Those fucking bastards!" Slade slammed his fist on the table so hard everyone in the cafeteria stopped and stared. He waved his hand for them to resume eating. "They're trying to make me look bad."

"This convoy is special. There's a doctor on board carrying blood samples that can be used to create a vaccine for the deader virus."

"Really?" Slade stroked his chin. "If we had those samples it would give us a lot of leverage over those government assholes. Why am I only hearing about this now?"

"Our source was on the train that dropped them off near Wichita. He just got back. They were picked up by that crew of geeks."

"Abney's people?"

Gina nodded.

"Any idea what route they're taking?" asked Mauler.

"That he didn't know."

"It doesn't matter. There's only one way to get to White Sands from the east. We can ambush them." Slade thought for a moment as he worked out a plan. "Mauler, how many deaders do we have in stock?"

"A little over a hundred that are armed."

"Load up fifty in the U-Haul. I want to be on the road in an hour."

"Can I make a suggestion?" asked one of the raiders.

"There's that new batch of deaders in Colorado Springs where the military base was recently overrun. Most of them are runners. It might give us an advantage."

Slade glared at the raider for a minute before breaking into a grin. "I like the way you think. Gibson, right?

"Yes."

"Take a tractor trailer and fill it with runners, then meet us at the ambush point on Route 380."

"The one near the quarry?"

"Yes."

Gibson nodded and stood.

Slade grabbed his arm. "And take the new bitch with you as bait. She's expendable."

As Gibson ran off, Slade focused on the others at the table. "Okay people. We move out in an hour."

A LITTLE OVER an hour later, two convoys left the Scavenger compound.

Slade led the first convoy from the Hummer H3. Gina, Mauler, and another member of his bodyguard unit rode with him. They were followed by a pair of two-and-half-ton National Guard trucks and the U-Haul truck packed with fifty deaders armed with necklace bombs. Slade turned south when he reached Route 87 and headed at top speed for New Mexico.

The second convoy consisted of a tractor trailer and two military Humvees commandeered from the Colorado National Guard. Gibson drove the lead Humvee. He brought seven raiders with him. The truck brought up the rear, with Wayne driving and Monica riding shotgun as bait. Once they reached Route 87, the second convoy veered right. It picked up Interstate 25 north of Pueblo and high-balled it for its destination – the North American Air Command (NORAD) in Colorado Springs.

Chapter Fifteen

M ONICA STARED OUT the window of the Mack, oblivious
to her surroundings. Wayne only told her why she had
been taken along once they passed Pueblo. Her task left her
numb. What he asked was suicidal. No, it went beyond that. It
was fucking insane. She had considered trying to wrestle the
Colt .45 semi-automatic pistol from his holster or grab the FAL
from the dashboard but thought better of it. She would never
be able to train the weapon on him in time to use it. The
thought had crossed her mind of jumping from the moving
truck and making a break for it, but what good would that do?
Even if she survived the fall without injuries, the two Humvees
would track her down and kill her. Her only chance of survival
would be to play along until she had a chance to escape.

After an hour drive, the convoy pulled up to the chain link
fence surrounding NORAD. Close to two hundred runners
milled around the main gate. On seeing the convoy approach,
they became agitated and swarmed against the fence. The
thought of running seemed much more appealing now.

Wayne did a three-point turn on the road and backed up to
within one hundred feet of the gate. Two raiders climbed out of
the Humvees and used the ladders welded to the side of the
trailer to climb on top. The Humvees withdrew a few hundred
feet down the road.

Wayne removed the Colt and handed it to Monica. "You
know what you have to do, right?"

"What if I refuse?"

"You're going to serve as bait either way. Whether you do it on your own or I shoot you in the leg and leave you in the front of the truck for the deaders to eat is up to you."

Monica took the weapon, opened the door, and got out. "Fuck you."

"Keep up that attitude, bitch, and I'll take you up on the offer once we get back."

Moving to the back of the truck, Monica pulled out the ramp used for loading the trailer, then unlatched and raised the door. She turned toward the main gate, mentally preparing herself for the next step.

"Hey."

Monica glanced up. The female raider set down her AK-47, slipped off her leather jacket, and dropped it onto the ramp. "It's not much, but it might prevent you from getting bit."

"Thanks." Monica put on the jacket and walked over to the gate.

The deaders surged forward, pushing against the gate, the only thing holding them back being the chain and padlock wrapped around the inner posts. Several bit the chain links trying to get at her, succeeding only in knocking out several of their teeth. Monica aimed at the padlock and fired four times. The first two shots missed. The third and fourth shattered the lock. With nothing holding them back, the deaders shoved the gate aside and swarmed after her.

Monica ran for the trailer, a mass of living dead chasing close after her. She reached another ladder welded to the front wall of the trailer and climbed. She made it halfway up when the first deader reached her, an MP with its shirt torn open and most of its guts missing. It grabbed her ankle and tried to pull her down. More deaders formed around the ladder, each one desperately reaching out for the fresh meat. She fired two rounds into the skull of the MP deader. Its head exploded and it released its grip. Monica climbed up onto the roof, collapsing on the metal surface and gasping from fear.

"Keep them occupied," yelled the male raider.

She leaned into the trailer, waving her arms and shouting, driving the deaders into a frenzy. In less than a minute, they packed the trailer to capacity. The remaining two dozen gathered around the opening or on the ramp, scratching and clawing to get inside. The raiders took down the excess with headshots, then switched out their magazines.

"You're up," said the male raider. "Don't worry. We have your back."

Monica detached a ten-foot pole with a hook on the end that had been latched to the roof. She climbed down the left-side ladder and approached the back, staying close to the trailer. Only now did she become aware of the stench of decay and the sound of hundreds of deaders snarling accompanied by the buzz of thousands of flies and wasps that fed off them. Reaching around the corner, she latched the hook through the strap hanging from the sliding door and closed it. Jumping onto the ramp, she slid the latch closed and secure it with a padlock from her pocket. Dozens of dead hands banged against the inside of the door trying to get out.

Monica leaned against the door and slid into a crouching position. Tears flowed down her face. Dear fucking God, she had survived.

The raiders climbed down from the trailer.

"What are you crying about?" asked the male. "You're still alive."

"Were you bit?" The female showed more sympathy.

Monica shook her head. "I'm fine."

"Then finish up and let's go. The Boss is waiting for us." He headed back to the Humvees.

The female helped Monica lift the ramp and slide it back under the trailer. When they were done, Monica slid off the jacket and handed it to her.

"Thanks."

"No problem. I've done this a few times myself." She put

on the jacket and held out her hand. "I'm Kate. The tight-assed one is Taylor."

"Monica." She shook the hand.

"You did good. Slade will be happy."

"I didn't do it for him."

"I know. But as long as you're of use to him, he'll keep you alive." Kate gave Monica a supportive squeeze on the shoulder. "Let's get going."

Back in the cab, Wayne held out his hand for the Colt. She gave the weapon back to him.

"You did good."

"Thanks." Monica forced a smile.

The three vehicles pulled away and headed down the road. Next stop, New Mexico.

Chapter Sixteen

EVERYONE GOT UP before dawn as the first rays of sun began to crest the eastern horizon. Breakfast was not as fulfilling as last night's meal, consisting of stale power bars and bottles of water. Lindsey took hers and went out to the barn. Alisa saw her a few minutes later walking the surviving horse around the corral.

It felt strange not being in charge and not having to do all the prep work before hitting the road. She loaded Archer in his carrier, which turned out to be almost as difficult as fighting off a horde of the living dead. He allowed her to cuddle and pet him. However, when she tried to put him in his cage, he struggled to break free. She always found it amazing how difficult controlling a sixteen-pound cat could be. Archer placed both front paws against the rim of the carrier and locked his arms, forcing Alissa to hold him in one hand and break his grip with the other. Finally, she got him inside. No sooner had she closed and locked the gate then he began whining and meowing to get out, an oldie but a goody.

Taking the carrier outside, she noticed everyone had boarded their vehicles except Nathan, Abney, and Lindsey. Kiera exited the bus and came over to Alissa.

"I'll take him."

"Thanks." Alissa handed her the carrier. "If he gives you trouble, place him near Shithead."

"Are you serious? He won't go near Archer even when he's locked up."

Alissa glanced around. "We forgot Thor."

"No. He's in the bus with the kids,"

"Good."

Kiera raised the carrier so she could see Archer. "Come on, Asshat. Time for another ride."

He let out a long, loud meow.

As Kiera went back to the bus, Alissa joined the others. "Sorry I'm late."

"Don't worry about it. Are we all set?"

The others nodded.

They climbed into the Ram and Abney started the engine. The convoy pulled away from the farmhouse. As they passed the corral, the horse stood by the fence, watching them forlornly.

"Stop for a minute," asked Lindsey.

Abney obliged.

Lindsey got out of the Ram and crossed over to the gate. The horse came up to her. She rubbed its nose for a minute, telling him everything would be okay. She kissed him on the top of the head and opened the gate to the corral so the horse would have a chance of surviving in the wild, then climbed back into the Ram.

The convoy headed out, turned left onto Route 50, and proceeded toward New Mexico.

THEY DROVE FOR five hours, finally stopping to rest on the New Mexico-Texas state line a few miles east of Nara Vista. Abney picked up the radio from the dashboard and pressed the talk button.

"We're taking a fifteen-minute break."

Everyone stretched. Shithead ran over to an old mailbox and did his business.

Carrington stepped off the bus. "It's good to get away from

that damn cat." He suddenly spotted Alissa and lowered her head. "Sorry. That was rude."

Alissa chuckled. "He's an asshat. I know. I live with him."

Kiera pointed ahead of the convoy. "What's that."

A quarter of a mile down the road, thirty-two white pigs, each weighing five hundred pounds or more, lumbered toward the group, probably having broken out from a nearby farm that the mailbox belonged to.

Susie squealed. "Oh my God. I've never seen a pig before."

"Can we pet them?" asked Connie.

Alissa glanced over at Abney, who shrugged. "I don't see why not."

"Leave the puppy here," said Lindsey. "He might scare them."

The kids handed the puppy to Kiera and ran off to the pigs. Patricia followed them.

"How long before we get to White Sands?" asked Carrington.

"Not long," Abney answered. "We just crossed over into New Mexico. We'll get you there before dark."

"Like we promised," added Lindsey.

The doctor sighed. "Good. I need to get these samples to—"

Shithead growled, a deep guttural sound that signified danger. His tail curled between his legs. His ears went flat and his fangs showed. Alissa followed the dog's gaze.

The threat came from the pigs.

Unslinging her Carbine, she ran toward Patricia and the kids.

"Get away from them! Now!"

PATRICIA PAUSED AND turned around to see what all the commotion was about. She saw Alissa and a dozen others running toward her, their weapons ready. Alissa and Lindsey pointed toward the pigs. She focused her attention back on the animals. Only then did she notice that they weren't right. The movement she had assumed to be waddling appeared more like a deader's shamble. As they drew closer, she saw the bite marks ripped out of their sides and the chunks of human flesh dangling from their mouths. The children were running right into certain death.

"Stop!" Patricia broke into a run. The children halted and looked at her. "Get back here now! They're deaders!"

Little Stevie realized the danger first. Taking the girls by the hands, he raced back to Patricia. Connie tripped and fell face first onto the ground. Little Stevie ran back to help her. Susie stood still, frozen in fear. Lindsey ran over, scooped up Susie in her arms, and rushed back to the school bus.

The first pig reached Connie and towered over her. She rolled over as it tried to bite her. She grabbed its snout, preventing the razor-sharp teeth from reaching her. She wouldn't be able to hold it back for long. Little Stevie ran up and grabbed its right ear, yanking to pull it away from Connie. The pig shifted its head and snapped at him, missing his arm by a few inches. Patricia used the opportunity to pull Connie away. The pig looked at them and snarled.

"Get out of the way!" yelled Joan.

Little Stevie retreated several feet while Patricia lay prone over Susie's body. Joan swung the axe like a baseball bat, severing the animal's lower jaw. Bringing the axe back, she swung it again, this time cleaving it in its eyes. The blade sliced deep, reaching its brain. It seized up.

A second pig climbed over the first and side checked Patricia, knocking her on her back. She felt her insides crushing under its massive weight. She screamed, unable to defend herself because of the pain wracking her body. It clamped its jaws around her neck and ripped it out, exposing her spine. Her cries became a gurgle as blood flowed into her lungs. Blood spurt from her severed arteries.

Alissa, Abney, Nathan, and Chris reached the battle site.

She fired at the pig's head. Because of the thicker skull, it took five rounds before the animal stopped moving and collapsed on top of its prey. Patricia met Alissa's gaze, her eyes pleading for mercy. Alissa shot her twice in the head.

"Get the kids out of here."

Nathan grabbed Connie and Little Stevie in his arms and rushed back to the others, most of who were coming to help. He passed the kids off to a terrified Miriam and Steve, then rejoined the others.

Kiera inserted herself between Alissa and Chris. They fired on the pigs approaching from the right. Off to the left, Abney aimed his revolver at a pig charging him, half its left flank eaten away. He fired six rounds before the animal collapsed and slid to a stop less than a foot in front of him.

At this rate, they'd be swarmed before they could defeat the pigs.

FIFTY-FIFTY JUMPED OVER the metal barrier surrounding the twin machine guns and swung them toward the pack. He couldn't take out those closing in on the others, but most of the pigs were wide open. He pressed the trigger.

The twin machine guns came to life, showering the outer fringe of the pack with fifty caliber rounds. Not even animals as huge as white pigs could survive the onslaught. The fusillade tore them apart. A mist of blood and gore formed in the air as the bullets found their mark. In less than a minute, twenty-two shredded carcasses littered the grass. Fifty-fifty shifted his aim to the remaining ones but couldn't fire because Abney and the others were in the way. Four pigs remained.

He prayed the others would make it out alive.

MOST OF THE others fell back one hundred feet, putting distance between themselves and the deader pigs. Abney reloaded his revolver. He didn't see the strategic retreat or the pig charging at him from his right.

"Pay attention," yelled Joan as she pushed him out of the way. He dropped his revolver and several rounds of ammunition.

Joan flung the axe at the animal. The axe missed its head, instead embedding in the small of its back near the spine, doing no damage. The pig ploughed into her, throwing her several feet onto her back and knocking the wind out of her. The creature straddled her, taking a bite out of her thigh. A bolt of pain worse than anything she had ever felt shot up her leg. Joan screamed, attracting two more pigs. One lumbered up and bent over her head. Its jaws opened and wrapped over her face, biting down hard. Its teeth punctured Joan's skin and dug into her skull. When it pulled back, it tore off the front half of her face, including her eyes. Joan's senses overloaded. Still, she kept up the fight. Unable to see, she lashed out in the blindness with her left hand, trying to punch the deaders. The third pig chomped down on her outstretched hand, biting off her fingers. It spit out the severed digits and attacked again, this time swallowing her arm up to the elbow and tearing it off.

Joan no longer felt pain or fear, her mind having completely shut down.

FIFTY-FIFTY SWUNG THE machine guns at the three pigs savaging Joan but couldn't fire on one of his own people.

"Put her out of her misery." The comment came from Pops, who stood beside the Jeep.

"But... Joan is one of us."

"Not anymore."

Fifty-fifty pulled the trigger. The twin machine guns came to life again. He concentrated first on Joan, pumping ten roads into her head and chest, then swung the weapon back and forth across the three pigs. He continued firing long after the animals were dead, pumping round after round into them and stopping only when the twin cases expended their ammunition. Left behind was a bloody heap of four unrecognizable bodies.

Fifty-fifty leaned over the protective wall and vomited. Pops said a prayer for him and Joan.

FIVE PIGS REMAINED.

Having safely gotten everyone on board the bus and closing the doors and checking that there was no danger coming from another direction, Tupoc and his team raced forward to help the others. Malcom joined them carrying a stun gun used in slaughterhouses to kill cattle before sending them down the line. He fired one bolt each into the skulls of the two closest pigs. One dropped instantly, stunned but not dead, its legs still kicking. The other let out an anguished oink and stood motionless, swaying back and forth. Tupoc raised his weapon, a World War II-era Thomas semi-automatic, and fired into their heads. Both pigs' skull exploded, covering him and Malcolm in blood and brain matter.

Alissa, Nathan, and the rest of Tupoc's team took down the last two pigs with little trouble, mass fire power making short work of them. An eerie silence fell over the area broken only by the swarms of flies that had started to feed off the bodies.

Carrington and Lindsey ran up, Lindsey hugged Abney. "I thought you were going to be eaten."

He hugged back and kissed her on the forehead. "I don't intend to be long pork for a pig.

"Are there any wounded?" asked Carrington.

Alissa shook her head. "How are the kids?"

"I checked them. Thank God none of them were bitten or scratched."

"W-what the fuck just happened?" stammered Malcolm. "Did the virus species jump?"

"I'm afraid so."

"You can't be serious," said Chris.

"I am." The doctor turned to Abney. "Have you encountered any other infected animals out here?"

"These are the first. Everything else we've run into has been normal."

"Then it's probably a fluke."

"What do you mean?" asked Lindsey.

"A pig's DNA is similar to that of a human. They can catch many of the diseases we can, including the common cold. It's only natural that the deader virus could be one of them."

"Shit," said Tupoc. "White Sands has been bringing in livestock from the surrounding areas."

"We'll warn them when we get there."

Abney interrupted the conversation. "Pack up, people. I want to get away from here as quickly as possible."

Everyone headed back to the convoy except for Abney. He made his way to the killing field and crouched in front of Joan's remains. Alissa watched as he bowed his head, said a silent prayer, and crossed himself. He did the same for Patricia.

Abney came back to the Dodge and silently climbed inside. No one spoke. He started the engine and pulled away, keeping his eyes fixed on the road.

Chapter Seventeen

T HE MORNING SUN hung low on the horizon. It had already taken the chill off the evening and, although still comfortable, promised to make the latter part of the day hot and unbearable. For all that Slade cared, the day could reach one hundred and twenty in the shade. By this time tomorrow, he would possess the one card that ensured victory in his political poker game with White Sands.

The one rule every terrorist and gang member knows is that the easiest place to hit an intended target is near their home. A cautious person could drive different routes every day to deter an enemy but could not avoid the inevitable choking point in front of their house. The same held true for White Sands. A secure military installation, there were only four entrances into the compound. The south and west gates would each add over a hundred miles to the journey from the St. Louis area and were deemed not worth the risk. The east gate bordered Alamogordo, which had fallen on day two of the outbreak. Any travelers taking that route would encounter tens of thousands of deaders. Which left only the north gate off Route 380. The route was sparsely populated so it had not been overrun by deaders, flat and open so there were miles of visibility, and possessed enough built-up locations perfect for an ambush.

Slade stood on top on one of those locations, scanning the surrounding area.

He had been smart enough to send out scouting parties to

survey the road, mostly families who had left one child behind at camp as a hostage. That way, if they stumbled into a military patrol, they would seem less suspicious, merely a family trying to survive. After two weeks of scouting, he had finally chosen the ideal spot – a natural roadblock two miles from Carrizozo. The right side of the road contained a ledge of rocks five feet in height and running fifty feet along the shoulder. It concealed anybody hiding along the northern side from the road and provided height to overpower their target. The left shoulder bordered a quarry and had not been maintained. A broken-down wooden fence and thick shrubs covered the area, making it impossible for any vehicle other than a tank or tractor to traverse it. When the time came, he would place the U-Haul truck across the road across the road at an angle so it blocked their passage and would release the mined deaders. The perfect ambush. One of his men on a motorcycle had been left at the eastern end of Route 380 to warn them when the convoy approached.

A rumbling came from the east. Slade used binoculars to check the horizon. Two Humvees led a trailer truck toward the others. Slade lowered the binoculars and climbed down from the rocky out crop to greet them. Gibson pulled up in the lead Humvee and stopped.

"Did you get them?" he asked.

"The trailer is full of them. All runners."

"Excellent." Slade pointed to a dirt road to the right of the outcrop. "We have all the vehicles parked at the end of this road where they can't be seen. Leave the Humvees and truck there and join us. Tell Jimmy and the others to wait for my signal to proceed."

"Yes, Boss."

Gibson led the three vehicles down the dirt road.

Slade crawled back on the outcrop and checked his watch. A little after eight. Now all he had to do was wait.

THE REST OF the trip passed without incident and without conversation, everyone mourning the death of Joan and Patricia. After traveling over three hundred miles they were all exhausted, edgy, and wanting nothing more than to reach the safety of White Sands.

"How much further?" asked Alissa.

"An hour," said Lindsey. "Maybe less."

"Thank God." Nathan leaned back in his seat.

INSIDE THE SCHOOL bus, most of the group had settled back for a nap. Little Stevie lay spread out on two seats in the left rear with Thor curled up in his arms. Susie and Connie sat in the seat in front of him, the latter resting her head on her friend's lap. Susie could not sleep, unable to get Patricia's death out of her mind. Kiera lay on the floor near the back, sound asleep, using a napping Shithead as a pillow. Rebecca sat in the seat in front of the girls to let them know she was there if they needed her. Miriam and Steve sat in the middle on the right side, Steve watching the countryside pass by and Miriam occasionally glancing over her shoulder at the kids. Carrington walked back and forth through the bus to stretch his legs. Kevin sat in the seat directly behind Kennedy, the driver, holding the cooler with the blood samples in his left hand. Chris sat in the back on the left side, his leg propped on the seat beside him. He stared down at Shithead, a little jealous but happy that his dog had become the protector of the kids. Archer lay in the carrier at his feet, being consigned to the back of the bus so the others didn't have to endure his endless whining. Thankfully, the cat had fallen asleep two hours ago.

TUPOC RODE HIS Harley along the left flank of the bus with

Liam behind him. Reg and Casey rode on the right flank. He looked forward to getting to White Sands. This had been one nightmare of a trip. He planned on treating his team to several rounds of beer until they had to be walked back to their bunks.

POPS DROVE AHEAD of the school bus in the left lane with Fifty-fifty seated beside him.

"What are you going to do when you reach White Sands?" Fifty-fifty asked.

"Sleep."

"Amen to that."

BRIAN BROUGHT UP the rear in the VW minibus. He wanted nothing more than a hot meal, a stiff drink, and maybe, if lucky, some female companionship.

MALCOM FOLLOWED BEHIND the Ram listening to a Led Zeppelin CD. Usually, he played music so he wouldn't fall asleep. Now he did it to keep his mind off what had happened earlier in the day. It was the first time they had ever lost a member and it hit him hard. He wondered how many more would be killed before this nightmare came to an end.

BADGER SAT IN a weathered wooden chair out in front of the general store. He had pulled the chair as close to the front façade as possible to sit in the shade, not wanting the sun to beat down on him for God knows how many hours. Badger pulled out a joint and smoked it, his third this morning. He could get away with it because he had the most boring assignment for this ambush – being the lookout for the approaching convoy.

The general store sat on Route 380 a mile northwest of Carrizozo, the small town the convoy would have to pass through on its way to White Sands. From here, he had a clear view of all the roads, including dirt trails in the desert, that converged on the town, giving him more than enough time to warn Slade to prepare the ambush. An easy enough task.

Except he had been doing it for almost seven hours. It re-minded him of that security guard job he had after high school watching a construction site overnight. The hardest part was not letting the boredom wear you down so you fell asleep. If he dozed off in the guard shack he'd be fired. If he dozed off and let the convoy slip past before he could warn Slade.... He would rather not think about that. But God damn, if something didn't happen soon, he would have to start jabbing the tip of his knife into his leg to keep—

A rumbling came from the east. At first, Badger thought it was wind blowing across the desert, only this sound remained constant and grew larger. Pushing himself off the wooden chair, he flung the joint into the sand and walked over to the end of the store. He raised a pair of binoculars and peered around the corner. The convoy they had been expecting barreled down Route 54 heading toward Carrizozo. A rigged up-Dodge Ram led the procession, followed by an ambulance, a school bus, and a VW minibus, the latter two having protecting coverings over the windows. A jeep and two motorcycles traveled along the bus's left flank as well as two more motorcycles on the right.

Badger pulled a radio from his pocket and keyed the talk button. "Boss, are you there?"

"I'm here. What's up?"

"The convoy we've been waiting for is heading toward Carrizozo. They should reach your position in less than ten minutes."

"What are we looking at?"

Badger gave his boss a breakdown of the convoy.

"Good job. Stay where you are and let me know if anything else comes our way. And if anyone escapes and heads your way, stop them."

"You got it, Boss."

Badger slid the radio back in his jacket, strolled back to the chair, and grabbed the AK-47 he had propped against the wall. Opening the door to the store, he slipped inside so no one would spot him. He had moved his Harley in here a few hours earlier. As he watched through the window, the convoy reached the edge of town, slowed to make the turn onto Route 380, then passed by him.

SLADE POCKETED THE radio and snapped his fingers at Tony. Tony raced up.

"Get the U-Haul out there now. The convoy will be here in a few minutes."

Tony ran down to the dirt road where the U-Haul was parked. Upon seeing him, the driver mouthed "Now?" Tony nodded and pumped his right fist. The driver crawled into the truck, pulled out onto Route 380, and headed west a few hundred feet before swerving right, stopping so the vehicle blocked both lanes. He shut off the engine, jumped out of the cab, and raced to the back where he unhooked the latch to the sliding door and slid it up. Before it opened all the way, the driver disappeared around the right side of the truck and circled back to the rocky outcrop. One by one, the mined deaders stumbled out onto the asphalt, struggled to their feet, and spread out across the road.

ABNEY ENTERED THE outskirts of Carrizozo and slowed the

Ram enough to make the right turn off Route 54 onto Route 380.

"We're in the homestretch," he said, a note of relief in his voice. "The entrance to White Sands is a few miles down this road."

"Thank God," muttered Nathan. "My ass feels like it's about to fall off."

"Don't get too excited," warned Lindsey. "We have a problem up ahead."

Chapter Eighteen

HALF A MILE down the road, a U-Haul truck sat at an angle blocking both lanes. The sliding door was open. A swarm of deaders milled around the immediate area. Upon hearing the approaching vehicles, they lumbered toward them.

Abney brought the convoy to a halt.

"Can we go around them?" asked Alissa.

Abney shook his head. "The grade of the shoulders is too deep. We'll make it, but the school bus will either get caught or tip over."

"What about using another road?"

"That'll mean going through Alamogordo at night, which you don't want to do."

Lindsey squeezed his hand. "We need to do something. I have a bad feeling about this."

Abney picked up the radio. "Malcolm."

The teenager's voice came over the radio. "Looks like we have a situation here."

"Circle around and lead them away from us so we can move the truck."

"Ah, the old Pied Piper. Will do."

The ambulance pulled away from the other vehicles, eased down the shoulder, and pushed its way through the living dead roadblock. Seven or eight shifted their attention to the moving vehicle and stumbled after it, scraping their hands and mouths against the side windows, posing no threat other than to leave smears of blood and gore across the glass. The rest continued shambling toward the rest of the convoy. Malcolm hugged the front fender of the U-Haul, scraping it along the right side of the ambulance. His left wheels became entangled in the brush along the shoulder. Malcolm pushed his foot on the accelerator. The ambulance lurched forward, breaking through. He veered back onto the road, stopping a quarter of a mile from the pack. Shifting into park, he made his way in back and sat in front of the stereo system, deciding which song to distract them with.

That's when all Hell broke loose.

ALL EYES WERE on Slade, waiting for his signal. He raised his left hand above his head, paused, then extended his forefinger and pointed to the top of the outcrop.

Slade and the thirty members of his team climbed onto the outcrop, aimed their AK-47s at the convoy, and fired.

MONICA SPUN HER head toward Route 380 at the sound of gunfire. The ambush had begun.

"Let's move," said Wayne.

Monica and Kate climbed up onto the top of the trailer and lay prone on the roof. Taylor went around to the back of the truck, undid the latch locking the sliding door in place, and banged on the door several times, driving the runners inside into a frenzy. When Taylor crawled onto the trailer, Wayne shifted into gear and headed for the main road.

CARRINGTON STILL PACED the aisle of the school bus. He glanced to his right as the Scavengers climbed to the top of the outcrop and raised their weapons.

"Everybody down!" the doctor yelled as he dropped to the floor.

Most of the gunfire was concentrated on the bus.

Being exposed on the right flank, Reg and Casey died instantly. Two dozen rounds struck them in the first two seconds, ripping them apart and destroying the twin Harleys. Neither realized what hit them.

Scores of rounds ricocheted off the steel plates welded to the side of the bus, sparing most of those inside. All the tires on the right side were blown out, immobilizing the vehicle. The rounds aimed at the windows shattered the glass and caused mayhem inside.

Steve pushed Miriam into the aisle and slid over to her seat. Before he moved more than a few inches, four rounds ripped through the wire mesh covering the windows and struck him, three in the back and one in the neck, blasting his head so that what little remained dangled onto his chest by a patch of skin still attached to the front of his neck. His body slumped over and fell on top of Miriam, protecting her even in death. Carrington crawled over and shielded Miriam's head.

The gunfire woke Little Stevie. He had enough sense to drop to the floor and curl into a ball, cradling Thor in his arms.

Kiera sat up with a start, watching bullets pass by overhead and exit out the windows on the other side. She rolled onto her side and wrapped her arms around Shithead who barked and tried to get into the middle of the fray.

Rebecca dived off her seat and covered the cat carrier. Three rounds went through the window she had been sitting in front of only a moment before.

Connie had been through enough that, at Carrington's warning, she hit the deck, missing being shot by a second. Suzie was not so lucky. Lost in thought and mourning her mother, she did not hear the doctor's warning. One bullet struck her in the right temple, splashing blood, brains, and pieces of skull against the wire mesh covering the shattered window. Thankfully, Susie died instantly.

Chris crouched and crawled across the aisle to the right

side of the bus, ignoring the rounds above him. He couldn't take aim without getting killed, so he placed the barrel of his Carbine on the bottom of the window and fired indiscriminately. None of the bullets found their mark, slamming into the rocky outcrop, though ricochets wounded two Scavengers, one in the chest and one in the leg.

STRAY ROUNDS THAT passed through the school bus, whizzing past Tupoc's and Liam's heads. They dismounted, grabbed their weapons, and ran over to the bus, hiding behind the rear and front tires, respectively. Tupoc attempted to peer around the back end to line up a shot, but a barrage of gunfire flew in his direction. He jumped back moments before being hit. Both men were now pinned down and unable to respond.

A BARRAGE OF AK-47 rounds slammed into the Dodge Ram. The rounds bounced harmlessly off the steel plates, saving the tires and those inside. Alissa and the others slid down into the seat wells. Several rounds shattered the windows, showering everyone in glass but, other than a few minor cuts, no one was hurt.

Abney grabbed the radio. "Get off the X now or we're all dead."

MALCOLM SAW THE ambush taking place in his rearview mirror. A dozen rounds tore into the back of the ambulance. He gunned the engine to get away from the barrage, spun left down the access road leading to the quarry, and parked behind an abandoned dump truck. Grabbing his weapon, he jumped out of the cab and made his way through the brush to provide cover fire for his friends.

He was unaware that three of the mined deaders had followed him down the road.

THE REMAINING DEADERS stumbled toward the convoy, attracted by the carnage. Half were cut down by the Scavengers and a dozen more were crippled, dropping to the ground and dragging themselves toward the food. The remaining ten shambled into the convoy. Most gathered around the Ram, reaching through the shattered windows at those inside. From their crouched positions, Alissa and the others used small arms fire to kill those that reached through the broken windows. Others were killed by the Scavengers firing on the Ram. Bodies fell to the ground, surrounding the pick-up.

BEING ON THE left flank of the bus, the Jeep was spared from the barrage of bullets. Fifty-fifty jumped out of the passenger seat and climbed into the back, climbing into the steel box surrounding the twin machine guns.

KENNEDY KNEW IF she didn't get out of there soon everyone would die. Despite the damage to the vehicle, she shifted into reverse and backed up. The bus moved slowly, shaking as the rims on the right side dug into the asphalt. She might have eventually made it to safety except that seven of the Scavengers concentrated fire on the front of the bus.

Over fifty rounds slammed into the engine, knocking it out of commission in seconds. The bus ground to a halt. A dozen rounds shattered the sliding door, most continuing on and ripping apart Kennedy, leaving behind a chewed-up body and a driver's compartment splattered with gore.

Three rounds passed through the forward most window, one slamming into the Plexiglas partition behind Kennedy and the last two punching into Kevin's back, smashing his left shoulder blade and puncturing his lung. He gasped for air as blood poured in.

A temporary lull settled over the area as the Scavengers reloaded.

"NOW!" YELLED FIFTY-FIFTY.

Pops accelerated, pulled in front of the bus, and stopped. Fifty-fifty swung the twin machine guns toward the top of the outcrop. The Scavengers were either busy reloading or concentrating their fire on the school bus. None of them were aware of the danger until Fifty-fifty squeezed the trigger.

The shells raked across the left end of the ridge with devastating effect, taking down seventeen Scavengers in two seconds. At this close range, those that were hit practically disintegrated. Limbs were blasted away and torsos ruptured like water balloons. A few attempted to take down the gunner, only to be blasted apart.

Those to the right of the ridge, including Yvette, seeing the line of bullets approaching, either jumped down on the other side of the outcrop or fell prone, keeping a low profile while returning fire. Slade was busy reloading and would have been cut down if Tony had not tackled his boss. Both men dropped into the desert, Slade bruising his left shoulder. Gina ducked and rolled, spreading out flat at the far end of the outcrop out of the line of fire.

WHEN FIFTY-FIFTY BEGAN his assault, Tupoc and Liam took advantage of the distraction. Stepping around the ends of the bus, they aimed at the few remaining Scavengers, picking off three and driving the rest back to the other side of the outcrop.

FROM HIS VANTAGE point on the other side of the road,

Malcolm sited in on a Scavenger lining up a shot on the Jeep. Malcolm squeezed the trigger and watched the gunman's head explode. He started to line up a second shot when a snarl came from behind him.

Malcolm glanced over his shoulder to see three deaders staggering toward him.

GINA RAN OVER to Slade and dropped to her knees. "Are you okay?"

"Nothing's broken." Slade sat up, wincing as pain shot down his left shoulder. She glared at Tony. "No thanks to you."

"I saved your life."

Slade ignored him. He withdrew the detonator from his pocket and passed it to Gina. "Blow them up."

Gina flicked the switch to arm the detonators.

The lights on forty-nine of the fifty mined deaders switched from red to green.

Gina pressed the detonator button.

THE DETONATORS IGNITED the primer chords that made up the collars. Forty-nine explosions rocked the area, the greatest concentration being from the deaders stacked around the Ram, although against the steel plating the charges did nothing more than shake the vehicle and splatter it with more gore. The remaining ones detonated far enough away from Abney's people that they posed no threat.

The collars on two of the three deaders stumbling toward Malcolm ignited, blasting off their heads. Malcolm walked over to the last one, raised his weapon, and dropped it with a double tap to the head.

None of Alissa's or Abney's people were hurt in the explosions. All it succeeded in doing was to distract them for a few precious seconds.

NONE OF THE Scavengers had directed any fire on the VW minibus at the rear of the convoy. Brian watched in shock at the slaughter taking place in front of him. Watching the Scavengers dive behind the outcrop to escape the machine gun fire snapped him back to reality and gave him an idea. If he could circle behind the outcrop, he could outflank the few remaining Scavengers.

Shifting into reverse, Brian began to back up but had to hit the brakes when a tractor trailer pulled out of the dirt road, cutting him off. It drove fifty feet and stopped.

Brian had a gut feeling this would not end well.

TUPOC SAW THE truck pulling out of the dirt road.

"Liam."

His friend crouched and came over, keeping his head below the steel plates on the bus. He spotted the trailer. "What's going on?"

"No idea, but it can't be good."

INSIDE THE BUS, Chris took advantage of the lull in the firing to reload and take up a position where he could fire on anyone who appeared on the ridge.

Rebecca grabbed her weapon and crawled over to the right side of the bus, taking a position in the third seat and, scanning the ridge top, waiting for the enemy to appear.

Miriam became hysterical, trying to get up, unable to do so because of Steve's body pinning her to the floor.

"Where's Steve?"

Carrington covered her head and prevented her from lifting it. "Stay down. The gunfire could start again."

"Where's Steve?"

"He's fine."

"I don't believe you."

"Mom," Little Stevie yelled. "It's okay. Stay down."

"Where's Kiera?"

"I'm fine," Kiera called from the back as she pulled her weapon from under the seat and crawled into a crouching position, ready to defend herself. "Stay where you are."

Miriam tried to break free.

Carrington pressed down even harder. "Please, stay still."

Miriam broke down in tears.

ABNEY AND ALISSA pushed open the doors on the Ram and jumped out, aiming at the outcrop while using the vehicle as cover. None of the Scavengers were visible.

"It's clear," said Alissa.

Nathan and Lindsey pushed opened the doors on the right, shoving deader corpses out of the way, and climbed out. Lindsey positioned herself between the front and rear doors, focusing on the ridge. Nathan heard the roar of the tractor trailer and glanced down the road. He mumbled to himself, "What new Hell is this?"

AS FIFTY-FIFTY KEPT his attention on the outcrop, Pop checked his rearview mirrors. He spotted the tractor trailer pulling onto Route 380. Shifting into reverse, Pops backed up a few feet until the bus was between them and the ridge.

"What are you doing?" asked Fifty-fifty.

"We may have a bigger problem." Pops pointed behind him.

When Fifty-fifty saw the truck, he swung the twin machine guns in its direction.

WAYNE STOPPED THE truck. Monica, Kate, and Taylor rushed along the roof of the trailer. The latter two fell prone, keeping their AK-47s trained on the convoy, searching for targets.

Monica removed the hook from its latch and laid prone, dangling over the end of the trailer. She slid the hook through the end of the strap and pulled it up, opening the sliding door.

One hundred runners flowed out of the rear of the trailer, tumbled onto the asphalt, and charged the convoy.

Chapter Nineteen

"I'M TOO OLD for this fucking shit."

Tupoc aimed his weapon at the horde and fired. Liam joined him. Attracted to the gun shots, the runners washed around the minibus like waves flowing around a boulder and charged the two men.

Kiera saw what was about to happen. She opened the rear emergency door. "Hurry up and get inside."

Neither needed further encouragement. Liam jumped in then turned around and helped Tupoc on board. The pack was ten feet away. Kiera fired into them, taking down the closest three, buying them a few extra seconds. With Tupoc aboard, Kiera closed the door, catching a dozen arms. The runners pulled on the door, opening it several inches. Tupoc and Liam grabbed on and pulled but were unable to close it. One runner started to crawl through, glancing up at Kiera and snarling. She slammed the heel of her boot into its face until she shattered the front of its skull and crushed its brain. The corpse slid out onto the road.

"We need help here," she yelled.

Chris left his position and raced to the back. "Let go of the door."

They did. The runners whipped it open. Chris emptied the magazine into the closest runners' heads, clearing the opening. Liam reached out and slammed the door shut. Kiera secured the lock.

The horde piled up behind the bus.

A SCAVENGER ROLLED over to the outer rim of the outcrop and got to his feet, looking for a target of opportunity.

Rebecca aimed at his leg and fired. The bullet found its mark. He dropped to his knees, screaming in pain.

As she had hoped, the yelling caught the attention of eleven runners. They stormed the outcrop and crawled up.

FIFTY-FIFTY SWUNG HIS twin machine guns toward the horde surrounding the bus and fired. Thirteen of the runners were ripped apart. The rest, sensing easy prey, rushed the Jeep. He continued firing, taking down another seven or eight before the twin cases ran out of ammunition.

The horde swarmed over them.

Pops didn't have a chance. Seven runners dragged him out of his seat and onto the ground, then began feasting. Four bit into each limb and a fifth his neck. The last two tore open his chest, ripping out one of his lungs and intestines, shoving the food into their greedy mouths.

The rest piled onto the rear of the Jeep trying to get at Fifty-fifty. He ducked down behind the steel barricade and curled up around the stand. Six of the living dead reached over the rim, clasping for him. He removed the .45 from his holster and fired a round into each of their heads. Five went limp, dangling over the side and preventing the others from getting at him. The sixth kept up the attack, only the top half of its skull gone. Fifty-fifty fired again, blowing off the rest of its head.

BRIAN BLARED THE horn on the minibus, hoping to attract the runners' attention. Only a handful responded, charging the VW and pouncing on the windshield.

ALISSA WATCHED IN horror as the runners ravaged their way

through the convoy. She raced over to the shoulder and fired at Pops. Five rounds walked their way down his body, putting him out of his misery.

The gunfire caught the attention of the gore-soaked runners feeding off him. They jumped to their feet and charged Alissa.

Nathan and Lindsey jumped back in the Ram while Abney provided cover fire for Alissa who ran back to safety. She jumped in beside Nathan. Abney followed, closing his door a second before the seven deaders, joined by ten others around the Jeep, swarmed the pick-up. Both couples hunched together in the middle of the cab, dead hands clutching at them through the broken windows. The four swatted at them with the stocks of their weapons.

"I think this is it," Alissa said to Nathan.

"We still have one option available." Abney pulled the radio off the dashboard. "Malcolm, are you there?"

THE ELEVEN RUNNERS who climbed the outcrop tore apart the Scavengers hiding on top who were not expecting the assault. Five noticed Slade and the others on the opposite side. Diving off the ledge, they attacked.

One charged Slade. Yvette placed herself between her boss and the living dead and fired. Her aim was off, the bullet passing by its head. It crashed into her, sprawling her on the ground and knocking the AK-47 from her hands. It sunk its teeth into her neck. Mauler rushed over, putting two rounds into the runner's head and one into Yvette's.

"We've gotta get out of here," urged Gina.

Slade raised his AK-47, taking down a runner. "We have nowhere to go."

Slade, Gina, Mauler, Tony and the last three Scavengers formed a line abreast, gunning down the runners around the outcrop.

"*MALCOLM, ARE YOU there?*"

He keyed his radio. "I'm here."

"We need you to lead these things away or we're dead."

"Roger that." Malcolm left his position on the shoulder and made his way back to the ambulance. He jumped in and began to circle back to the main road, then stopped. The quarry lay three hundred yards to his left. He had an idea.

"Abney, any chance you can lead those things to me?"

"I think so. What do you have in mind?"

"Just lure them in here."

"I hope you know what you're doing."

I do, Malcolm thought to himself.

Turning the steering wheel left, he made his way to the opposite side of the quarry.

ABNEY REMOVED THE revolver from his holster and fired two rounds into the head of the runner reaching through the side window. Holding it in place with his left hand so nothing else could reach him, he slid over into the driver's seat and shifted into drive. He surged ahead until the Ram lay between the U-Haul and the shoulder, then blared the horn.

Every runner still alive, those on the minibus, those behind the school bus, and those swarming the Jeep raised their heads, searching for the sound. Abney blared the horn again, this time keeping his hand pressed against it. Noise meant humans, and humans meant food.

As one, the remaining deaders, numbering just under sixty, broke into a run for the Ram.

Abney gunned the engine and pulled away, the steel plates on the right side of the pick-up scraping against the U-Haul's fender. Once certain he was clear, Abney continued down the main road, still blaring the horn and driving slow enough that none of the runners would lose sight of him.

He turned onto the dirt road leading to the quarry and

stopped two hundred feet in front of the pit. The runners were right behind them.

"Let's hope this works," said Abney.

"Let's hope what works?" asked Alissa.

Lindsey shifted in her seat and smiled. "Just watch."

MALCOLM STOOD OUTSIDE the ambulance, relieved when he saw the Ram pull into the quarry with the runners chasing after him. He acknowledged Abney with a wave then crawled in back, stepped over to the stereo system, and hit Play. He jumped outside to watch.

Led Zeppelin's *The Immigrant Song* blasted from the roof-mounted speaker. The twin cry of the Viking yell blared over the compound. The runners ignored the Ram and rushed the ambulance, not noticing the open quarry in front of them.

We come from the land of the ice and snow
From the midnight sun where the hot springs flow.

The first seven runners reached the rim and kept going, sailing off the edge and plummeting into the rocky bottom one hundred feet below. Their bodies ruptured on impact. Only three died immediately, the rest remaining semi-alive but with crippled bodies, posing a threat to no one.

We'll drive our ships to new lands
To fight the horde, sing and cry
Valhalla, I am coming.

The rest of the runners followed like lemmings, going over the rim to shatter on the rocks below. Within seconds, all but a handful had gone over the side, the few that remained slowing down, uncertain whether to proceed.

The Viking yell blasted through the speaker again, animating the last runners. They dashed forward, dropping over the edge to join the pile of bodies at the bottom of the pit.

Crawling back into the ambulance and closing the doors behind him, Malcolm shut off the stereo, climbed into the driver's seat, and drove over to the Ram. He parked by the driver's side, a huge grin on his face.

"I told you it would work."

Abney grinned back. "I never doubted you."

Alissa leaned out. "That's the best deader kill I've ever seen."

Malcolm beamed. "Thank you."

"Let's check on the others," said Lindsey.

FROM THE ROOF of the trailer, Monica watched as the runners were led away by the Ram. From her vantage point, she observed the ambulance lure them into the quarry. They had failed. Though she would never admit it, she was glad.

Taylor did not feel the same way. "I don't fucking believe this."

"What now?" asked Kate.

Taylor ignored her and radioed Slade.

MIRIAM FELT THE blood pouring from Steve cover her back and spread across the floor. "I want to see Steve and my kids."

"I'm okay," Little Stevie called from his hiding spot, still clutching Thor against his chest.

"Stay down, Mom." Kiera kept her eyes open for deaders. "We're still in danger."

"Steve?" Miriam called out.

No answer.

"Steve!"

Carrington hugged her as best he could. "I'm sorry,"

No." Miriam's voice broke.

"Your husband died saving your life."

"No. He's only wounded." She tried to get up but Carrington wouldn't let her. "I want to see him."

"It won't do any good. Please."

"No." Miriam tried to get up again, this time half-heartedly, eventually stopping. She broke down, her tears mixing with her husband's blood.

Little Stevie slid across the floor, holding the puppy in his right hand. He took his mother's hand in his left, squeezing gently and telling her it would be all right.

SLADE HEARD TAYLOR'S voice over the radio. "Boss, are you there?"

"What the fuck is going on?"

"They cleared out the runners. There's still a bunch alive inside the bus. What do you want to do?"

"We can charge them and overpower them," urged Mauler.

"They have the advantage and we don't have enough men."

"You're not going to let them get away with this, are you?"

"Shut up!" Slade contemplated his next move.

Taylor's voice came over the radio again. "Boss, are you—"

A gunshot rang out from the other side of the outcrop.

KIERA SAW THE Scavenger standing on the back of the truck talking into a radio. She pushed open the emergency door halfway, lined up her shot, and fired.

"BOSS, ARE YOU—"

A single round struck Taylor in the chest. He dropped the radio on the roof and tumbled off the side, landing headfirst on the asphalt.

Monica and Kate fell prone. Kate crawled over to the radio and picked it up. A second round passed overhead.

"Boss, they're firing on us. What do you want us to do?"

INCREASING GUNFIRE CAME from the other side of the ridge. Slade had played enough poker to know when to fold. He keyed the radio.

"Tell Wayne to back the truck up. We're getting out of here. You and Taylor give us covering fire."

"Taylor's dead. We'll come and get you."

Fuck, thought Slade. He turned to the others. "Head for the truck."

"What about our vehicles?" asked Gina.

"We'll have to leave them." No one moved, each of them too stunned at having been defeated. Slade grabbed Gina by the arm and pushed her. "Go."

THE TRUCK'S BACK up signal sounded. It reversed gears and backed down the dirt road.

Kiera, Tupoc, and Liam fired at the truck, trying to pick off the two remaining Scavengers on the roof, but they hugged the deck and no shots found their mark. Chris lined up at the far end of the trailer, hoping to get a shot at the driver. The driver partially backed the trailer down the dirt road, never exposing the cab to gunfire.

When they saw the Scavengers climbing on board the trailer, they concentrated their fire in that direction.

SLADE REACHED THE trailer and helped Gina on board, then jumped on himself. As he climbed inside, a bullet struck him in the left leg, passing through flesh and tissue before exiting on the other side.

Hearing the cry of pain from his brother, Mauler rushed forward, pushed Slade to safety, then crawled inside after him.

Tony and the other three followed.

When everyone was inside, Monica crawled to the front of the trailer and yelled for Wayne to go. He shifted into drive and pulled away. One of the Scavengers grabbed the clasp and began lowering the rear. Four streams of gunfire slammed into the metal. Three rounds hit the Scavenger in the chest and groin, the latter slicing open an artery. The remaining bullets ricocheted around inside the trailer, none of them finding a target. Monica and Kate made their way to the interior ladder and joined the others inside.

Wayne drove down Route 380 to Carrizozo, turned left onto Route 54, and headed back to base.

Chapter Twenty

THOSE FROM THE quarry arrived back at the convoy in time to watch the Scavengers escape. No thought was given to chasing them. There were too many of their people to attend to.

Alissa, Nathan, and Abney jumped out of the Ram and rushed over to the school bus. Tupoc and Liam had already jumped out, the latter checking on Reg and Casey. Tupoc headed over and intercepted Abney.

"How bad is it?" Abney asked.

"We lost Kennedy." Tupoc shifted his attention to Alissa. "Three of yours were killed."

"Who?"

"Kevin, Steve, and one of the kids."

"Which one?" Alissa didn't wait for an answer.

She raced around to the emergency door, running into Chris and Shithead who jumped out onto the asphalt. She circled around them but Chris stepped in front of her.

"It's bad. Suzie and Steve were killed along with Kevin and Kennedy."

"Any other casualties?"

"Thank God, no." Chris leaned closer so no one could hear him. "Miriam is having a breakdown. Kiera, Little Stevie, and Rebecca are trying to comfort her."

As she climbed aboard the bus, Chris and Shithead joined Tupoc and Liam in checking the outcrop for survivors.

Miriam sat on the floor, cradling the mangled body of her

husband in her lap. Blood stained her clothes and hands and fed a growing pool of crimson. Rebecca rested on the seat behind Miriam, her hands on the grieving woman's shoulders. Little Stevie sat beside his mother, hugging her. Kiera knelt by her father, crying over his corpse. Connie sat on the chairs across from them, holding Thor in one arm and clasping Suzie's dead hand in the other.

Alissa moved over to Miriam and crouched beside her. "I'm sorry."

Miriam swallowed hard, trying to control her crying. "It's not your fault. It's this damn outbreak."

She broke down again, holding the body closer. Alissa placed her hand on Miriam's back, comforting her as she cried.

LINDSEY RAN OVER to check on Pops. Malcolm rummaged around in the ambulance for the first aid kit and then followed her, though the kit would be of no use. Between the feeding and the gunshots that put him out of his mercy, not much recognizable remained of the body.

"We got our asses handed to us," said Malcolm.

"I can't believe we lost so many—"

A moaning came from the Jeep. Lindsey and Malcolm raised their weapons. The pile of deaders around the steel cage moved. Malcolm raised his weapon to fire but Lindsey placed her hand on the barrel and pushed it down. One by one, the deaders fell aside, collapsing off the vehicle. A moment later, Fifty-fifty stood up, covered in congealed blood and gore that dripped off him. He shook his head, flinging off the human detritus.

"This is disgusting."

"Hang on." Malcolm ran back to the ambulance and returned a moment later with a sheet, which he handed to his friend. "Clean yourself off with this."

After Fifty-fifty toweled off his upper body, Malcolm helped him out.

Sirens came from the west. A moment later, two military Humvees with flashing blue lights and the letters MP painted on their hoods raced up and stopped near the U-Haul. Eight military police in full battle gear jumped out, four forming a perimeter defense while the others rushed over to Lindsey.

"Is everything okay?" asked a lieutenant with the name BRONSON embroidered on his chest patch.

"We're fine," she replied. "We were attacked by Scavengers but they retreated. They left a few minutes ago and are heading east on 380. You might be able to catch them."

"No can do, ma'am. Our orders are to bring you in."

"We should be ready in a few minutes," said Lindsey. "Help those on the bus."

THIRTY MINUTES LATER, they were ready to head to White Sands. The bodies of Steve, Suzie, Pops, Kennedy, Reg, Casey, and Kevin had been transferred to the front end of the U-Haul and covered with whatever was available. The passengers aboard the bus, including the three pets, rode the rest of the way in the truck. Miriam sat up front, crying and holding Steve's lifeless hand.

The bus and two of the Harleys were damaged beyond repair. The military would return in a day or two to remove those vehicles, confiscate those the Scavengers had abandoned, and throw the deaders into the quarry with the others. The clothes and bodies of the Scavengers would be thoroughly searched for anything of intelligence value then dumped with the other corpses, a fate most at White Sand believed was too good for them.

Bronson stood by the rear of the U-Haul. "Are we ready?"

"Give me a minute," said Malcolm.

The teenager climbed into the ambulance and drove back to the quarry site, heading for the location where the three deaders had attacked him. Getting out, he stepped over to the one whose collar had not exploded. He broke off a branch from a nearby shrub and used it to pull the collar off the deader's severed neck, all the time watching to make sure the red light didn't turn green. Using the branch, he placed the collar on the floor of the ambulance by the stereo then rejoined the others.

The convoy set off for White Sands with Bronson's Humvee in the lead and the second bringing up the rear.

Thirty minutes later, it turned off Route 380 onto a paved road heading into the desert. After a mile, they reached the northern gate to White Sands which now served as the main entrance to the facility. One hundred yards from the gate, a trench had been dug five feet wide and ten feet deep with sharpened wooden spike like *pungi* sticks lining the bottom. Two M1 Abram tanks sat between the trench and the fence. Two soldiers opened the gate. When the convoy was through, it stopped. A female sergeant approached the Ram.

"Welcome to White Sands. Sorry to hear what happened back there."

"That's okay," said Abney. "At least we made it."

"Some of us made it," added Alissa.

The sergeant nodded her understanding. "If you'll please follow Lieutenant Bronson, he'll take you to the quarantine facility where you'll be checked for wounds and held in confinement for twelve hours."

"None of us were bitten," said Alissa.

"SOP for all newcomers, ma'am." Though her expression was friendly, the sergeant's tone made it clear skipping confinement was not an option.

SLADE SAT ON the examination table in Vestas' medical facility, fussing and fuming as Dr. Berson checked his bullet wound.

I can't believe we got our asses handed to us by a bunch of assholes." He slammed his elbow against the table.

"Calm down," advised Gina.

"Don't tell me to calm down, you stupid bitch." He swung out his left hand, slapping Gina in the face.

Doc threaded a hooked needle. "Boss, you'll need to lay still so I can stitch the wound."

Slade glared at the doctor but gave in to common sense. "How bad is it?"

"You lucked out. It's only a flesh wound. It'll hurt like a son of a bitch for a week, but I can give you drugs for that. Another two inches to the left and the bullet would have shattered the bone, or worse, hit your artery."

"Hurry and patch it up."

Tony leaned against the wall by the door to the examination room. "I know we suffered a setback—"

"Setback? We lost a lot of good people out there plus all our vehicles."

"They can be replaced. Besides, it doesn't alter our plans."

"You're an optimistic bastard," snarled Slade.

"I'm telling the truth."

Slade calmed down a bit. His second was right. Today didn't alter the future. It only made the next step in their takeover of the area that much more fulfilling.

"How close are we to completing stage one?"

"A couple of days. Right on schedule."

"Send out a crew in the morning to pick up some more deaders. We need to beef up our stock…. What's the fucking needle for?"

Doc held a syringe in his right hand. "It's Lidocaine. It'll numb the area around the wound so you don't feel me stitching it up."

"Go ahead." Slade returned his attention to Tony. "You take care of everything and make certain we're ready to go in three days."

"No problem, Boss."

Slade laid back on the table, psyching himself up for the stitches, constantly reminding himself that the payback against White Sands would be one vengeful bitch.

MONICA LAY IN the top bunk staring at the ceiling. She had been a captive of the Scavengers for only a few days and had experienced more nightmares than she had since the outbreak began. The were no deaders to arm so she had the night off. Devon warned her a squad would go out tomorrow afternoon to get more, so tomorrow night she would be working overtime. Based on what little she knew about Slade, he wouldn't stop until he enacted revenge for their loss earlier today.

Monica doubted she would make it out alive.

EARLY THE NEXT morning, Alissa's and Abney's people gathered at the makeshift cemetery at White Sands. The military had dug seven graves for their fallen comrades and buried the bodies. The mourners stood by the mounds paying silent respect as *Amazing Grace* performed by bagpipes softly played from the ambulance speakers. Abney gave the benediction.

"Heavenly Father, accept the souls of our departed friends into the Kingdom of Heaven and embrace them with Your love and care. Please also look after their loved ones left behind. Comfort us in the knowledge that their untimely demise was not in vain but the result of doing Your work in this deader-infested wasteland. Help us to deal with our grief and heartache. Bless us with Your grace and keep us safe. In Your name we pray. Amen."

When the service was finished, Miriam stepped forward,

fell to her knees in front of Steve's grave, and sobbed. Kiera, Little Stevie, and Connie comforted her. The others made their way back to the vehicles.

Alissa inserted herself between Abney and Lindsey. "What are you planning on doing now?"

"We haven't thought about it," said Abney.

Lindsey agreed. "With a third of our people and vehicles gone, we're not much use as an escort service for the military anymore."

"I was hoping you'd stay around and help me."

The other two stopped. Abney asked, "What are you going to do?"

Alissa took two steps and turned around to face them. "I'm going after the Scavengers."

PREVIEW OF *NURSE ALISSA VS. THE ZOMBIES VIII: NEW BEGINNING*

A LISSA WOKE UP to an entirely new life. The months she and the others had spent in the cabin in New Hampshire, surviving the outbreak and thriving, were now in the past. Reality warned Alissa she would ever return there. After the attacks on or near the cabin, the retrieval mission into Boston to get Dr. Edwards' blood for a possible vaccine, the outbreak on Warren Island, and the disastrous journey across country to get here, today marked a new chapter and hopefully more positive chapter in their lives. This morning she began a new day in her own room at White Sands.

"Her own room" was an exaggeration. Eleven thousand two hundred and fifteen people now resided at the installation, putting living space at a premium. Only the acting president and the general in charge of White Sands had private quarters. Alissa shared a bunk with the other women from her group – Miriam, still in mourning over the death of Steve, Kiera, Rebecca, Connie, and Thor, the Labrador puppy. The men shared another room in the male section of the housing dorms. Little Stevie opted to stay with Nathan, Chris, and Shithead, beginning his transition from childhood to being an adult. Dr. Carrington joined the medical staff in a separate building. Abney's escort team had quarters reserved for them down by the motor pool. After the ambush just miles from White Sand, there were far fewer of Abney's people than usual.

Alissa tried to swing her legs out of bed but couldn't. A meow greeted her efforts. Archer lay curled up at the end of the bed, cuddled against her. He raised his head and stared at her, his tail swishing.

"I know it's not as nice as your cabin, but at least it's safe and it's home."

Archer meowed again. She gently pushed him three times with her leg before he finally stood, stretched dramatically, and jumped off the bed to snack on the bowl of salmon-flavored treats she had laid out for him last night.

"Well, someone is finally up," said Kiera. She sat on her bunk playing with Thor.

Alissa smiled and lovingly raised her middle finger.

Kiera placed Thor on the floor. Yipping and with his tail wagging, the puppy raced over to make friends with Archer. The cat ignored him, intent on eating. Thor wrapped his paws around Archer's tail and playfully nipped at it. Not pleased with the attention, Archer spun around and wacked Thor three times on the head. The puppy yelped and ran back to Kiera, who picked him up and hugged him.

"Did that mean old cat beat you up?"

Thor yipped.

Rebecca chuckled. "It's nice to see that some things haven't changed."

"Yeah," Alissa sighed. "Archer will always be an asshat."

Miriam lay on her bunk facing the wall.

"How is she doing?" Alissa whispered to Kiera.

"Not good. She's taking dad's death pretty hard."

"Are you okay?"

"I miss him a lot, but I have to stay strong for mom."

Alissa hugged her. Kiera had grown up so much in the last few months.

"Have you had breakfast yet?"

"Rebecca and I took Connie down an hour ago. Mom didn't want to go."

"How's the food?"

"It's fucking awesome." Kiera spoke it out loud, especially

the swear, hoping to get a rise out of her mother. Miriam remained silent and stared at the wall.

Alissa sat on the end of Miriam's bunk and placed a hand on her leg. "Why don't you have breakfast with me? I could use the company."

"I'm not very sociable right now."

"Are you sure?"

"Yes. Leave me alone."

Alissa had witnessed more than her fair share of grief working in the ER. The worst part of the job was having to inform loved ones that a patient had died. Over time, she had learned to emotionally detach herself from such situations while maintaining a professional façade of caring and understanding. She had to otherwise the grief would have driven her insane. This instance was different. She knew Steve personally. Had escaped from Nahant with him, lived with him, fought beside him, and watched him die. Because she forced everyone to leave the cabin for New Mexico, a part of her felt responsible for Steve's death, as well as that of Patricia and Susie. Alissa prayed Miriam didn't feel the same way.

"You stay here and rest. Let me know if you need anything."

Miriam did not respond.

Alissa rose and walked over to Kiera. "I'm going to breakfast. We'll give your mother time to grieve."

Kiera mouthed "Thank you."

Alissa left.

EVEN AT NINE in the morning, the line for the mess hall stretched outside the building and around the corner, which was to be expected considering the number of people to be fed. The military had done an incredible job under the circumstances. The aroma reached her before she got inside. She took a ladle of scrambled eggs with ham, home fries, sausage, orange juice, and coffee. If breakfast tasted half as good as it looked and smelled, this would be a delightful meal.

Once outside, she found her guys seated at one of fifty picnic tables spread across the parking area, each with its own umbrella. Shithead saw Alissa and barked to get her attention. She joined them and sat down beside Little Stevie.

"I see you guys are doing nothing, as always."

"I don't start work until this afternoon," said Nathan.

"You have a job?" Alissa asked, a confused tone in her question.

Nathan frowned. "We all do."

"Everyone here has to contribute." Chris slid a piece of paper across the table.

Alissa picked it up and studied it. It contained a list of names of those from her group. Nathan had been assigned to the security detail for White Sands. Rebecca would help in the day care unit. Miriam would work in the makeshift school as a teacher. Even Little Stevie had an assignment.

She nudged Little Stevie. "Looks like you'll be going back to school."

"I know," he responded sullenly.

Alissa wrapped her arm around his shoulders, pulled him close, and kissed the top of his head.

"I have double duty," Nathan added unenthusiastically. "According to Dr. Carrington, the blood samples we retrieved broke down and can't be used to develop a vaccine."

"Are you fucking serious?" Alissa spat out the words loud enough for those at the nearby tables to hear, including the children. Embarrassed, she raised her hands and looked at the others around her. "Sorry. Please forgive me."

Everyone went back to eating, though several families grumbled their discontent.

"You mean we went through all that in Boston... lost all those lives... for nothing?"

146

Chris frowned. "I'm afraid so."

"Fuck." This time Alissa said it under her breath.

"There is a positive side," added Nathan. "Carrington says since I fought off the deader virus my blood can be used to make an antidote for anyone who gets bit. It's not as good as a vaccine, but at least it gives anyone infected a fighting chance."

"At least it's something."

"I'll be a human guinea pig by day and a security officer at night."

Chris slapped his friend on the shoulder. "See, there are advantages to being Patient Zero."

Nathan glared at his friend.

Alissa went back to reading the paper. Her, Chris, and Kiera were on the list but with no jobs assigned to them. "Why aren't we included?"

Chris grinned. "Abney has requested the three of us join his team."

A Thank You to My Readers

I've been writing for as long as I can remember. It's one of the most fulfilling things I've done with my life. I love sitting on my front porch or in my back yard, surrounded by nature while writing, often with Walther and Bella sitting beside me or getting into trouble.

The best part is having fans who read my books and enjoy them. I'm extremely fortunate and grateful that I have a fanbase that devours my novels like zombies eating human flesh. You keep reading and I'll keep writing.

If you liked *Nurse Alissa vs. the Zombies VII: On the Road,* or any of the other books in the series, please post a review on Amazon. It doesn't have to be long—just a rating and a sentence or two about why you enjoyed it. The more reviews the series receives, the more opportunity other readers have of discovering the book.

The *Nurse Alissa* saga will continue. The next book in the series is currently in production and the plans are to make Alissa's life miserable well into 2021, maybe even 2022. I have some unique situations planned for Alissa's team and some interesting characters they'll run into.

A new series, which is more along the lines of clean para-normal romance/horror, is going well. *The Ghosts of Eden Hollow* is already in print and the sequel, The Ghosts of Salem Village, is in production a 1 June release. In addition, plans are moving ahead on that non-zombie, post-apocalypse series I was talking about earlier.

So, hang on. This year is going to be exciting.

Acknowledgments

Writing is solitary and lonely. Getting a book published is a complicated process involving many people, all of whom deserve to be recognized.

I want to thank my Beta readers, the unsung heroes of writers. No matter how many times you edit and proofread your manuscript, errors always slip through. My Beta readers, especially Dan Uebel and Doc Fried, provide detailed notes on the spelling, grammatical, or punctuation mistakes I missed and help me not to look illiterate.

Christian Bentulan designed the cover art for *Nurse Alissa vs. the Zombies VI: Rescue* as well as the other books in the saga. I love Christian's work. His covers reach out and grab the reader's attention as well as foreshadow what is to come within the pages.

You would not be reading this book, or any of the others in the *Nurse Alissa* series, were it not for my dear friend and colleague, Alina Giuchici. I hadn't written a zombie series since *Rotter Apocalypse* was published in 2015. Alina is a major fan of my stories and kept urging me to go back to writing about the living dead. With some gentle shoving in the right direction and a few well-placed ideas, over the course of a long week on the road I came up with the concept of the Alissa series. If you like these books, be sure to thank Alina.

Finally, a major debt of thanks goes to my family, human and furry. As with my last seven novels, I wrote, edited, and released this one during the COVID-19 outbreak, taking advantage of having so much time on my hands and being stuck at home. This has been the best year of the dogs' lives because they think I stay home all day to be with them, and they want to spend every minute with me. The cats are pissed off that I'm around all the time, especially Archer whose naps are disturbed by my typing. (Yes, Alissa's Archer is taken directly from my own cat Archer, especially his asshattery.) It's hard to maintain my writing discipline when everyone is home, and even harder to maintain my sanity when there is nowhere to go, but I couldn't do this without their love and support.

About the Author

Scott M. Baker was born and raised in Everett, Massachusetts and spent twenty-three years in northern Virginia working for the Central Intelligence Agency. Scott is now retired and lives just outside of Concord, New Hampshire with his wife and fellow writer Alison Beightol, stepdaughter, two rambunctious boxers, and two cats who treat him as their human servant. He has written seven books in the *Nurse Alissa vs. the Zombies* saga, his latest zombie apocalypse series; *The Ghosts of Eden Hollow*, the first book in his clean paranormal romance series; the *Shattered World* series, his five-book, young adult post-apocalypse series about a group of adventurers attempting to close portals into Hell; *The Vampire Hunters* trilogy, about humans fighting the undead in Washington D.C.; *Rotter World*, *Rotter Nation*, and *Rotter Apocalypse*, his first post-apocalyptic zombie saga; *Yeitso*, his homage to the giant monster movies of the 1950s that he loved watching as a kid; as well as several zombie-themed novellas and anthologies.

Please check out Scott's social media accounts for the latest information on future books, upcoming events, and other fun stuff.

Blog: scottmbakerauthor.blogspot.com
Facebook: facebook.com/groups/397749347486177
MeWe: mewe.com/i/scottmbaker
Twitter: twitter.com/vampire_hunters
Instagram: instagram.com/scottmbakerwriter

You can also receive his newsletter by signing up at
mailchi.mp/0b1401f1ddb2/scott-m-baker-writer

www.ingramcontent.com/pod-product-compliance
Lightning Source LLC
Chambersburg PA
CBHW050736230626
47052CB00002BA/399